Acting Edition

Packing Up Polly

by Leslie Kimbell

Copyright © 2024 by Leslie Kimbell
All Rights Reserved

PACKING UP POLLY is fully protected under the copyright laws of the United States of America, the British Commonwealth, including Canada, and all member countries of the Berne Convention for the Protection of Literary and Artistic Works, the Universal Copyright Convention, and/or the World Trade Organization conforming to the Agreement on Trade Related Aspects of Intellectual Property Rights. All rights, including professional and amateur stage productions, recitation, lecturing, public reading, motion picture, radio broadcasting, television, online/digital production, and the rights of translation into foreign languages are strictly reserved.

ISBN 978-0-573-71111-4

www.concordtheatricals.com
www.concordtheatricals.co.uk

FOR PRODUCTION INQUIRIES

UNITED STATES AND CANADA
info@concordtheatricals.com
1-866-979-0447

UNITED KINGDOM AND EUROPE
licensing@concordtheatricals.co.uk
020-7054-7298

Each title is subject to availability from Concord Theatricals Corp., depending upon country of performance. Please be aware that *PACKING UP POLLY* may not be licensed by Concord Theatricals Corp. in your territory. Professional and amateur producers should contact the nearest Concord Theatricals Corp. office or licensing partner to verify availability.

CAUTION: Professional and amateur producers are hereby warned that *PACKING UP POLLY* is subject to a licensing fee. The purchase, renting, lending or use of this book does not constitute a license to perform this title(s), which license must be obtained from Concord Theatricals Corp. prior to any performance. Performance of this title(s) without a license is a violation of federal law and may subject the producer and/or presenter of such performances to civil penalties. Both amateurs and professionals considering a production are strongly advised to apply to the appropriate agent before starting rehearsals, advertising, or booking a theatre. A licensing fee must be paid whether the title(s) is presented for charity or gain and whether or not admission is charged. Professional/Stock licensing fees are quoted upon application to Concord Theatricals Corp.

This work is published by Samuel French, an imprint of Concord Theatricals Corp.

No one shall make any changes in this title(s) for the purpose of production. No part of this book may be reproduced, stored in a retrieval system, scanned, uploaded, or transmitted in any form, by any means, now known or yet to be invented, including mechanical, electronic, digital, photocopying, recording, videotaping, or otherwise, without the prior written permission of the publisher. No one shall share this title(s), or any part of this title(s), through any social media or file hosting websites.

For all inquiries regarding motion picture, television, online/digital and other media rights, please contact Concord Theatricals Corp.

MUSIC AND THIRD-PARTY MATERIALS USE NOTE

Licensees are solely responsible for obtaining formal written permission from copyright owners to use copyrighted music and/or other copyrighted third-party materials (e.g. artworks, logos) in the performance of this play and are strongly cautioned to do so. If no such permission is obtained by the licensee, then the licensee must use only original music and materials that the licensee owns and controls. Licensees are solely responsible and liable for clearances of all third-party copyrighted materials, including without limitation music, and shall indemnify the copyright owners of the play(s) and their licensing agent, Concord Theatricals Corp., against any costs, expenses, losses and liabilities arising from the use of such copyrighted third-party materials by licensees. For music, please contact the appropriate music licensing authority in your territory for the rights to any incidental music.

IMPORTANT BILLING AND CREDIT REQUIREMENTS

If you have obtained performance rights to this title, please refer to your licensing agreement for important billing and credit requirements.

PACKING UP POLLY received its world premiere production at OnStage Atlanta in Scottdale, Georgia on April 9, 2021. The show was directed by Barry West. The Stage Manager was Meghan Zern. The scenic design was by Barry West. The lighting design was by Harley Gould. The sound design was by Sylvia Veith. Costume design was by Scott Rousseau. The cast was as follows:

CAROLINE PORTER COOK	Marita McKee
ELIZABETH JENNINGS	Irene Polk
DONNA JO MARTIN	Cat Rondeau
REBECCA BAILEY	Kelley Gray

PACKING UP POLLY received a rewrite and second premiere at Winder-Barrow Community Theatre in Winder, Georgia on October 14, 2022. This production was directed by Leslie Kimbell with Assistant Director Ann Mitchell. The Stage Manager was Savannah Hardegree. Scenic design was by Leslie Kimbell and Ann Mitchell. Lighting and sound design was by Aaron Mitchell. Costume design was by Eddie Nadeau. The cast was as follows:

CAROLINE PORTER COOK	Léland Downs
ELIZABETH JENNINGS	Andrea Barra
DONNA JO MARTIN	Bryn Adamson
REBECCA BAILEY	KAT Marie Mitchell

CHARACTERS

CAROLINE PORTER COOK – 40s – Polly's daughter – former Head Cheerleader, Homecoming Queen, Prom Queen, and all that goes with it.

ELIZABETH "LIZZY" JENNINGS – 40s – Caroline's high school best "frenemy." Owner of the Miss Georgia Belle pageantry system.

DONNA JO MARTIN – 40s – Drama queen, local theatre diva and one-time Off Off Broadway actor. Married eight times.

REBECCA "BECCA" BAILEY – 40s – Frumpy mother of four...currently expecting number five any minute...and soon to be single.

SETTING

The den and kitchen area of Polly Porter's ranch style home – Savannah, Georgia.

TIME

Spring – 2015.

AUTHOR'S NOTES

The set should be very heavily cluttered with...well...clutter. Cardboard boxes, newspapers, clothing on coat hangers hanging in the doorways, shopping bags, odd out-of-place items, stacks of mail and shipping boxes, multiple televisions, an ironing board, a Christmas tree, misplaced furniture, overflowing shelves...etc. This all strikes during intermission. Though never used, it can be quite impactful to have a door stage left in the kitchen area that is fully blocked with all the hoarding and is only revealed after intermission. In Act One, Scene Two, the effect of the pull-out sofa is dynamic, but it is not absolutely necessary to have a pull-out sleeper sofa. Instead, sleeping bags, pillows, and blankets will work.

Have fun with the odd and bizarre hoarded items.

For the gospel music, the author suggests a song in the style of "Looking for a City" by Vestal Goodman. However, a license to produce *Packing Up Polly* does not include a performance license for this music. The author suggests using other up-tempo gospel songs for scene transitions.

For Eddie Nadeau
Who told me I wasn't an imposter...
and made me believe in myself.
I love you forever.

ACT ONE

Scene One

(Lights up.)

(We are in the den and kitchen area of a modest open-concept ranch home, built in the late '60s.)

(The décor consists of faux wood-paneled walls, accented with orange and avocado green. A plaid pull-out sleeper sofa is center. Stage left is a small kitchen area with a refrigerator, a few cabinets, and a simple 1970s dinette set. The table is loaded with casserole dishes, pies, and colorful, well-used Tupperware. Stage left is a door that leads to the formal part of the house, but we can't yet see it as it has chairs, boxes, and other items stacked in front of it. Upper center is a small, raised area with a brown wood railing and the back door that opens to the carport. Stage right is a cased opening into a hallway leading to the bedrooms and bathroom. There is a bookcase overly filled with books, record albums, framed photos, and mementoes. In the living area, there is an old console-style stereo with built-in record player. A rotary phone sits on the end of the console. There is a real feeling of being in the '70s.)

(There is heavy clutter everywhere...stacks of boxes, mail, magazines, decorations for several different holidays, newspapers, blankets, books, dolls, odd out-of-place items, knick-knacks and multiple unopened shipping boxes. The walls are covered with pictures and art. Clothing hangs on metal coat hangers in the hallway opening. Someone lives here...someone who likes to keep things...a hoarder.)

*(**CAROLINE PORTER COOPER** enters. She is well put together, dressed in black, and carries a tote bag. She is talking on a cellphone.)*

CAROLINE. ...of course I'm not surprised... Chelsea has always been self-centered...and Michael...well...all I can say is...bless his heart...ya' know? *(Laugh.)* God help me, I love my baby brother...even though he *may* or *may not* be a gambling-addicted grifter. *(Beat.)* Oh yes...yes... He ran out of the church so fast he nearly knocked over the minister. *(Beat.)* No...she stayed for the whole service...but she kept looking at her watch. The second Pastor Wofford said the last Amen, she got up and ran out the side door. *(Beat.)* I have no idea where she is. (**CAROLINE** *calls out.)* CHELSEA?! *(Beat.)* CHELSEA? *(Beat.)* Well...she's not here. *(She crosses to the kitchen.)* Lord have mercy, you should see all this food...there's enough Kentucky fried chicken in here to sink the *Titanic*...and *(She opens a container and smells it. She scowls.)* I don't have any idea what some of this stuff is. *(She looks under the container for a label.)* Lord have mercy, this is Lucy Jenkins' Nine Bean Fiesta Salad...it would gag a maggot! *(Beat.)* Of course I appreciate it...but who's gonna eat it?

(She drops the container into a nearby trashcan.)

Looks like it's just gonna be me here. Lord only knows how long this is all gonna take...Momma is such a pack rat *(Beat.)* was...*was* such a pack rat.

> *(**CAROLINE** crosses to the sofa and sets down her tote. She is suddenly overcome with grief and it registers on her face. She sits...barely holding herself together.)*

Listen honey... I've gotta go...yes I'm fine...no...no... I just need to...you know...get myself together...and I need to call Patrick too...and I've got to run over to the Piggly Wiggly or somewhere and get some boxes. *(Beat.)* Oh...it's a grocery store. *(Beat.)* No really... I'll be fine. I'm gonna try to get this done and be back to Atlanta next week...there's a lot I have to deal with there too. Thank you for taking care of everything on that end. *(Beat.)* Yes... I promise I'll call you tomorrow... *(Beat.)* OK sweetie... I've gotta go...bye.

> *(She hangs up, looks around the room and begins to softly cry.)*

Oh Momma –

> *(She reaches into her tote bag and pulls out a tissue. She then pulls out a small cardboard box and sits it in her lap. These are Polly's ashes.)*

Well...here we are... I can't believe it. *(Beat.)* Oh, Mommy this can't be real...what am I gonna do without you? I need you. Who am I gonna talk to about Patrick? *(Beat.)* How am I gonna reconnect with the girls...like we planned? We were gonna do it together... I can't do it by myself...oh Momma I need you to tell me what to do...send me a sign or –

> *(There is a quick knock on the front door and **ELIZABETH "LIZZY" JENNINGS** enters. She is a peppy and perky beauty pageant*

professional, perfectly dressed in a twinset, skirt, heels, and pearls. She carries a designer purse and a "to go" Styrofoam food container. She wears pearls and a Miss Georgia Belle nametag. **CAROLINE** *is shocked to see* **LIZZY**...*and vice versa.*)

LIZZY. Yoo hoo Miss Polly...it's Elizabeth... I brought you some meatloaf from Earl's –

CAROLINE. Oh my God –

(**LIZZY** *stops dead in her tracks.*)

LIZZY. Caroline?

CAROLINE. Lizzy?

LIZZY. Oh my God –

CAROLINE. Oh my God... Oh My God –

LIZZY & CAROLINE. What are you doing here?

LIZZY. I came to check on Miss Polly.

CAROLINE. What? Why are you checkin' on my –

LIZZY. Wait what's going on Caroline...where's Miss Polly... is she OK? *(Realization.)* Oh no –

(*Beat.*)

CAROLINE. Lizzy... Momma died.

LIZZY. Oh, Caroline...no –

(*Beat.*)

CAROLINE. Mommy died.

LIZZY. Oh Caroline...no... I don't believe this... I am so sorry.

(**LIZZY** *rushes to* **CAROLINE** *to hug her and stops short. It is an awkward moment.*)

CAROLINE. Did you say you were checkin' on my momma?

LIZZY. Well yes, I've been checkin' in on Miss Polly for years...didn't she tell you? I love your sweet momma. She's like a second momma to me...to all the girls. I come by and bring her dinner sometimes too.

CAROLINE. *(Soft.)* No...no...she never told me.

>   (**CAROLINE** *sits the box of ashes on the coffee table.*)

LIZZY. I have been over in Valdosta all weekend with the Little Miss Georgia Belle pageant. I can't believe nobody called me. Oh Caroline, when did this happen?

CAROLINE. Sunday night. *(Beat.)* Chelsea came over Monday to check on Momma...which is of course her code for "ask for money" and she found her. *(Beat.)* Momma just went off...and died in her sleep.

LIZZY. Oh Caroline, I am so sorry...but I am so glad it was peaceful...that's a real blessin'. That's how I want to go –

CAROLINE. *(Tearful.)* Yeah –

LIZZY. How old was Miss Polly?

CAROLINE. *(Smiling through tears.)* Well, if you asked her...she was fifty-nine *(Giggle.)* but she was really seventy-eight. *(She looks up.)* Sorry Momma.

LIZZY. I just can't believe no one called me... I am so sorry I missed the service.

CAROLINE. We didn't have much of a service, really. The obituary doesn't even go into the paper 'til tomorrow... and there hasn't been a press release...so none of her old fans know yet. Michael didn't get here 'til this mornin' ...so we just had a small service at the funeral home. Most of Momma's really *good* friends are already gone. It was nice though...they played some of Momma's music –

LIZZY. Oh, that's sweet Caroline.

CAROLINE. It was just –

> (**CAROLINE** *is lost in emotion.* **LIZZY** *senses and changes the subject.*)

LIZZY. Now where did you do the service? Not Williams Brothers, I hope.

CAROLINE. No... I used Owens Funeral Home.

LIZZY. Thank God...did you know those Williams boys have started doing *theme* funerals.

CAROLINE. Theme funerals?

LIZZY. Yes! They have a receiving room called, Granny's Kitchen...and you can have your sweet Mee-Maw laid out right in the middle of a kitchen setting...stove, refrigerator, and all.

CAROLINE. NO! That's awful...*really*?

LIZZY. IT IS! I was there last week... Tootie Jackson passed...rest her soul...and people were just standin' around eatin' cake over her body...with a pot of beans on the stove...and a big ole' skillet of cornbread on the table.

CAROLINE. You can't be serious –

LIZZY. Yes it was awful...tacky, tacky, tacky! And listen to this... Freddy Tillman passed back in February...rest his soul...and Mavis had him laid out in their *Man Cave* theme room.

CAROLINE. I shudder to ask...

LIZZY. YES! She had him laid back in a recliner, with a Georgia Bulldogs game playin' on a big screen TV. He was wearin' his old flannel pajama pants and a NO FAT CHICKS T-shirt...remote control in one hand and a beer in the other. *(Beat.)* Everybody said he looked so natural.

CAROLINE. That sounds dreadful.

(Pause.)

LIZZY. It was. So...where are Chelsea and Michael?

CAROLINE. Who knows? *(Beat.)* I haven't seen or heard from either one of them in over two years...until this. I'm surprised they even called me...well actually...no I'm not...they *do* want someone to clean out the house.

LIZZY. Clean out the house? *(Beat.)* This house?

CAROLINE. Yes...they want to pack up the whole thing and get it ready to sell...as soon as possible. Chelsea wants to donate *everything* and put it on the market by next weekend.

LIZZY. *Next* weekend? That's fast –

CAROLINE. Well...the faster we sell it...the faster Michael can get to the casinos in Biloxi...and Chelsea...well... I'm sure she will use her share to have somethin' lipo-sucked, tucked, or implanted –

LIZZY. Aren't they comin' to help you?

CAROLINE. *(Snicker.)* I *highly* doubt it...they said *WE* need to get the house packed up...and then they both disappeared. So, as usual... I guess it's up to me to deal with all the hard stuff. . I've done it all our lives...why should this be any different?

LIZZY. Well now honey...who is the executor of the estate?

CAROLINE. Estate? Oh Lizzy...that's funny...Momma didn't have a pot to pee in –

LIZZY. That can't be true. Surely Miss Polly must have a will or somethin'. I mean...after all those concerts and record sales...and all those years tourin' with the band? Polly Porter and the Praise His Name Singers were the top tourin' gospel band of the seventies and eighties.

CAROLINE. I don't know...Momma and I didn't talk about money and that sort of thing... I guess I thought she was gonna live forever. *(Beat.)* I just don't know what I'm gonna do –

(**LIZZY** *awkwardly touches* **CAROLINE***'s shoulder.*)

LIZZY. When's the last time you saw Miss Polly? She just came up to see you didn't she?

CAROLINE. Yes...she flew up to Atlanta last month, for a few days...but we talked on the phone all the time. I mean... I just talked to her Saturday mornin'...and she sounded great.

(**CAROLINE** *dazes off.*)

LIZZY. Caroline, Miss Polly is so proud of you.

CAROLINE. What do you mean?

LIZZY. She talks about you all the time...nonstop.

CAROLINE. Really?

LIZZY. She brags on you...about your big fancy job at that Investment Bank...and Patrick. Hey...where *is* Patrick? Is he here?

(**LIZZY** *rises and looks around.*)

CAROLINE. *(Uneasy.)* Oh, no...he had this big business thing in California and couldn't get away.

LIZZY. *(Puzzled.)* He couldn't get off work to come to your momma's funeral?

CAROLINE. It's a deal that has been in the works for a year...and it could mean a big promotion.

LIZZY. *(Skeptical.)* Uh huh...okay –

(Awkward beat and then a change.)

Listen sweetie... I know this is strange...me showin' up here and all out of the blue...but why don't you let me help you out around here? I've got three weeks until my next pageant...and... I would like to help you get through some of this...if you'll let me.

CAROLINE. Oh Lizzy... I... I don't know –

LIZZY. Caroline... I know we've had our differences...but I really want to help.

CAROLINE. Well –

LIZZY. Let's just let...bygones be bygones. Besides darlin'...there is *no way* you can do this by yourself.

CAROLINE. Thank you Lizzy...that would be...nice... I really appreciate it.

(**CAROLINE** and **LIZZY** *take in the room.*)

LIZZY. Lordamercy I feel like I am steppin' back in time when I come here –

CAROLINE. I know...there are so many memories. It hasn't changed a bit since we were kids. Well...except maybe all this...um...clutter.

(**CAROLINE** *wipes her eyes. There's a change in her voice.*)

Well... I'm gonna go change out of this dress. You hungry?

LIZZY. No...not really –

CAROLINE. There's enough food in the kitchen for fifty blue million people. If you *get* hungry...make a plate or two...or three...in fact...go out and feed the homeless... there's enough porkchops and sweet potato pie in there for everybody in Savannah.

(**CAROLINE** *exits right.*)

LIZZY. Thanks honey but I just ate lunch at Earl's place.

CAROLINE. *(Offstage.)* I can't believe they brought so much food from the church.

LIZZY. Well...you know how us Southern Baptists are about death and hospitality...we want to make sure you've got enough fried chicken and green beans while you're mournin' your loss. God forbid you be sad *and* hungry.

> *(As soon as **CAROLINE** exits, **LIZZY** takes out her cellphone and makes a call. Her voice is low.)*

LIZZY. Hello... Donna Jo? It's Lizzy. Did you know that Polly Porter got on the Jesus bus? *(Beat.)* Yes...it's awful... I just came by to see her and found out...*from Caroline. (Beat.)* Yes... I'm here right now. *(Beat.)* Yes, I'm serious. *(Beat.)* What are you doing right now? *(Beat.)* Dress rehearsal...for what? *(Beat and scowl.)* Oh. Well...get your booty over here to Miss Polly's ASAP. Caroline has to pack up Miss Polly's whole house and she is gonna need help...it's a long story... oh and listen...call Becca and see if she can come help too. *(Beat.) I know that*...but she can be moral support *(Beat.)* What? No, I didn't tell her I was callin' you... I just want y'all to show up. I'll confess later. Oh, oh she's comin'...gotta go...bye.

> *(**CAROLINE** enters in sweatpants and a T-shirt as **LIZZY** tucks her cellphone back in her bra.)*

That was fast.

CAROLINE. Were you on the phone?

LIZZY. Yeah... I just called Bobby to let him know he'll have to heat up leftovers for dinner tonight.

CAROLINE. Tonight? You're stayin' *now*?

LIZZY. Well of course...someone has to help you plan...and you know how I love to make lists.

CAROLINE. Oh...well thank you Lizzy... I don't know what to say –

LIZZY. Just say thank you and let's get goin' ...where do you want to start? I guess we need to make a game plan.

(**CAROLINE** *is overwhelmed.*)

CAROLINE. Well... I don't know...there's just...so much stuff... 'specially in the back of the –

(**LIZZY** *gets a pad and pen from her purse.*)

LIZZY. Okay...let me go look in the bedrooms...while you get your thoughts together.

CAROLINE. I'm not sure I'm ready to...I mean... You may want to wait before –

LIZZY. *(Ignoring.)* I'll make a list of the supplies we need... and then I'll make a run for some boxes...and tape –

CAROLINE. Well... I...think that –

LIZZY. *(Pacing.)* And then we'll just go room-to-room and pull things out and make decisions... I mean... I'm sure there's some things you'll wanna keep...like pictures and mementoes and so forth...and then we can always donate the rest of the stuff over to the church thrift store or the Goodwill...whaddaya think?

CAROLINE. OK...but...maybe you should –

LIZZY. I watch those home organizing shows all the time on HGTV...so this is gonna be a snap. Ooooo...maybe we can have a little estate sale thingy on Saturday? Whaddaya think?

CAROLINE. Estate sale? Uh...well... I suppose we *could consider* –

LIZZY. I've got some folding tables I use for the pageants at home... I'll call Bobby and get him to bring 'em over here to set up on the carport... I need to let him know I'm not comin' home for dinner anyway.

CAROLINE. Lizzy I think we need to slow it –

(**LIZZY** *exits right.*)

LIZZY. *(Offstage.)* OH MY WORD CAROLINE –

CAROLINE. I tried to warn you.

LIZZY. I haven't looked back here in years. These rooms are packed floor to ceilin'! Good Lord, where did your momma get all this stuff? *(Beat.)* And why in the world did she need one...two...eight...ten... *THIRTEEN* cases of Kotex at her age? I know her cousin hasn't visited in thirty years. This is crazy!

(**LIZZY** *returns.*)

We're gonna have to get a dumpster. I'll call Elmer over at the sanitation department and get one sent over... maybe two.

CAROLINE. WHAT? Lizzy...slow down...wait...did you say you were callin' Bobby? Didn't you already call Bobby?

LIZZY. *(Caught.)* What? Oh yeah...that's right... I did, didn't I? *(Beat.)* Dammitt! *(Beat.)* Oh alright...listen... I called Donna Jo and asked her to come over here and help us.

CAROLINE. WHAT? Lizzy...*no*...*why?* This is just too much... I'm not ready to see her –

LIZZY. Honey you need us right now...and there is no way we can do this by ourselves...have you looked in there? I've never seen anything like it.

CAROLINE. Well...Momma liked to collect stuff –

LIZZY. It looks like she's *collected* most of Savannah and half of Jacksonville.

CAROLINE. Momma never threw *anything* away.

LIZZY. Caroline...there are two sets of snow tires in there... and at least six *brand-new* toaster ovens...piled on the bed...at least I think it was a bed...and there's got to be a hundred boxes from QVC and Amazon that haven't even been opened.

(They wander to the food table.)

CAROLINE. Yes... I know Lizzy... Momma liked huntin' for bargains and stuff...yard sales...thrift stores...and then she started orderin' stuff on the computer too –

LIZZY. Sweetie... Miss Polly was a hoarder –

CAROLINE. I don't like that word Lizzy...but she –

LIZZY. Oh honey...you weren't kiddin'...look at all this food...what's this? *(She lifts the lid and scowls, then looks at the label on the bottom.)* Lordamercy...it's Janelle Tucker's Meat Surprise. I'm tellin' you right now...the *surprise* is when someone actually eats it... and lives.

CAROLINE. Oh, I know...close it...*close it*... I might start gaggin' –

*(**LIZZY** reaches for a trashcan and **CAROLINE** tosses the entire casserole in the trash.)*

LIZZY. *(Brightly.)* Well...look at us...we're already makin' progress.

*(The home telephone rings and **CAROLINE** crosses to retrieve it.)*

CAROLINE. Hello. *(Straining to hear.)* Chelsea... CHELSEA IS THAT YOU? *(Getting louder.)* WHAT? WHAT IS THAT NOISE? *(Beat.)* What? Well I'm sorry Chelsea... I must have my ringer turned off. Where are you? *(Beat.)* At the airport? *(Beat.)* Where are you goin'? *(Beat.)* I can't understand you. HELLO? Where's Michael? WHAT? CHELSEA? HELLO? ...HELLO?

(**LIZZY** *grabs the phone.*)

LIZZY. Hello Chelsea? You better get your fanny over here... Hello... *(Beat.)* Did she hang up on you? That girl never did have a single lick of manners in her life! Where is she goin'?

CAROLINE. I *think* she said Las Vegas! No wonder she ran out of the church so fast –

LIZZY. Las Vegas?

CAROLINE. *(Sigh.)* Yes...she has a new man in her life... he's older than Methuselah...he's in his eighties...come to think of it...he and Momma went to high school together.

LIZZY. *(Scowl.)* Nooooo

CAROLINE. And rollin' in the dough...we're talking *old* Southern money...you know what I mean...*sugar daddy* money.

LIZZY. OK...that's just gross. *(Beat.)* Do you think they... uh...you know...bow chicka wow wow?

CAROLINE. *(Shock.)* LIZZY! I don't *even* want to think about it. *(Beat.)* She's my sister and I love her...even if she is a lazy, gold-diggin' hussy who'd sooner cut off her own arm than do an honest day's work.

LIZZY. Don't hold back Caroline...tell me how you really feel.

(**LIZZY** *passes another food container to* **CAROLINE**.)

CAROLINE. *(Snicker.)* I believe I just did.

(**CAROLINE** *looks in the container and gasps.*)

LIZZY. What?

CAROLINE. Do not eat this! This is Annie Mae Zorn's Ambrosia, and everyone knows she uses canned grapefruit –

LIZZY. NO!

CAROLINE. Yes! Canned! I mean...how hard is it to peel a fresh grapefruit? *(Realization.)* Oh, my Lord... I sound just like Momma –

LIZZY. Yeah...sometimes I open my mouth and my momma comes flyin' out too –

> *(Without discussion,* **CAROLINE** *and* **LIZZY** *begin to open cabinets and take things out as they talk...stacking or tossing. They pull out a few extremely unusual items that would not traditionally be kept in a kitchen cabinet. They pause briefly and stare at each other and the items they are holding...then slowly put the items down and continue without comment.)*

CAROLINE. How are your twins doin'...they must be graduatin' soon.

> *(***LIZZY** *beams.)*

LIZZY. Oh...they're *perfect*...absolutely *perfect*. My Ricky and Mickey are the two most perfect boys God ever created. They graduate in May. *(She looks in a container.)* Do you think I ought to put this salad in the fridge?

(She crosses to the fridge.)

CAROLINE. If you can find room...there's at least five macaroni salads in there... I don't know *how many* Jell-O salads...and a truckload of Kentucky fried chicken.

LIZZY. Maybe I'll just take some of this food home for Bobby and the boys –

CAROLINE. I already told you...take it home...take it *all* home...please –

(A change.)

LIZZY. *(Angry.)* You know the more I think about it... I cannot believe that Chelsea and Michael have put all this on you. I am so mad right now... I could just spit –

> (**LIZZY** *slams the salad container down.*)

CAROLINE. Calm down Lizzy...don't get started up like you always –

LIZZY. I mean...who do they think they are, leavin' all this for you to do by yourself?

> (**CAROLINE** *crosses to the living room.* **LIZZY** *follows with the kitchen trash can. She randomly tosses old magazines, newspapers and knick-knacks in the trash.*)

CAROLINE. They've been this way since we were kids... I mean...you know...Momma was gone with the band so much...so I practically raised 'em. They never learned a lick of manners. What are you throwing out?

LIZZY. It's just trash...well...it just ticks me off to no end... I mean they're just so selfish and greedy –

> (**LIZZY** *picks up Polly's ashes to toss in the trash.* **CAROLINE** *reaches out in panic.*)

CAROLINE. LIZZY NO... STOP!

LIZZY. What?

CAROLINE. Lizzy...that's Momma –

LIZZY. *(Confused.)* Excuse me?

CAROLINE. That's my momma –

> (**LIZZY** *looks at the box and then back at* **CAROLINE** *in shock.*)

LIZZY. WHAT? *(She drops the box with a bang on to the table.)*

CAROLINE. LIZZY!!

(There is a quick knock on the door and **BECCA BAILEY** *rushes in. She is nine months pregnant and a train wreck. She wears no makeup, and her hair is a mess. Her mismatched clothes are wrinkled.)*

BECCA. Hello? Caroline? Liza-beth? I'm here –

CAROLINE. *(Confused.)* Rebecca? Hi...what are you doing here?

*(***LIZZY*** sits on the sofa, picks up the box of ashes and stares at it.)*

BECCA. Oh Caroline... I'm so sorry... I can't believe Miss Polly is gone... Donna Jo called me, and I ran right over.

*(***BECCA*** embraces ***CAROLINE***, who glares at ***LIZZY***.)*

CAROLINE. *(Strained.)* Oh *good*... Donna Jo called you... well...isn't that sweet?

LIZZY. Caroline...why is Miss Polly in this little cardboard box?

BECCA. *(Horrified.)* Miss Polly is in a box...what?

CAROLINE. She was cremated Lizzy...those are her ashes *(Then to* **BECCA.***)* Mommy was cremated...they gave me her ashes today.

LIZZY. Well, I know *that* Caroline...but why isn't she in somethin' nice...like a pretty urn...or *somethin'*? I mean... I just about threw your sweet momma into the trashcan.

*(***CAROLINE*** *takes the box and puts it back on the coffee table.)*

CAROLINE. Lizzy...the service was just this mornin'... I haven't had a second to find an urn...all the ones at the funeral home were tacky...nothin' looked like... Momma –

BECCA. Oh Caroline... I just don't know what to say.

(**CAROLINE** *hugs* **BECCA** *and notices her pregnancy.*)

CAROLINE. Becca...look at you...you're pregnant...*again*.

BECCA. Yep.

CAROLINE. Is this number four?

BECCA. Five.

CAROLINE. FIVE!?

LIZZY. Yeah...she decided to get in one more, just under the wire.

BECCA. Under the wire?

LIZZY. Well honey...we're not spring chickens...our eggs *do* have an expiration date ya' know.

BECCA. Yeah... I thought my last few remainin' eggs were powdered...but as it turns out...they're still farm fresh... *(Smiling.)* dang it.

LIZZY. Doctor Dixon says it's a *geriatric* pregnancy.

BECCA. Makes me feel like Grandma Moses.

LIZZY. So...are there any other loved ones sitting around in little cardboard boxes I need to know about?

CAROLINE. Um...no –

LIZZY. Great –

(**LIZZY** *resumes gathering items to throw out.*)

I just don't know how Becca's gonna to do it all alone.

BECCA. LIZZY!

CAROLINE. Alone? Why alone?

LIZZY. Oh honey... Tucker and Becca Bailey are gettin' a D-I-V-O-R-C-E.

CAROLINE. Oh no Rebecca...what happened?

(**BECCA** *glares at* **LIZZY**.)

BECCA. Well...a few months ago... Tucker went through a midlife crisis...so he went out and got that love handle liposuction and those... Botox face injections.

LIZZY. It's *awful*...he looks like this –

(**BECCA** *and* **LIZZY** *make a crazy, wide-eyed surprise face...and then laugh.*)

BECCA. Then he went off and bought this little red sports car. He said he wanted to try and "find himself"...but instead, he went out and found Tiffany...the slutty homewrecker. *(Beat.)* She sold him the car.

LIZZY. *(Sarcastic.)* She's like what...fifteen?

BECCA. May as well be –

LIZZY. Her boobs are *enormous*...bigger than Dolly's.

BECCA. I don't know how she can stand upright, without tippin' over.

CAROLINE. Oh Becca... I'm sorry –

BECCA. Don't be... I'm not. Tucker Bailey is just a big ole butthead –

LIZZY. And she is takin' everything... EV-REE-THING!

CAROLINE. When did all this happen?

BECCA. 'Bout a month or so ago... Lizzy saw him over at the –

LIZZY. *(Quickly interrupting.)* I was in the Burger Barn drive thru gettin' Momma a hamburger when I saw 'em. At first I thought he was bein' attacked by a wild animal. I was just about to call 911...until I saw her big ole' red push up bra hangin' on the rear-view mirror.

CAROLINE. Oh no!

LIZZY. So, I ran over to his car window and yelled... BUSTED! He just about had a heart attack. *Then* I took a couple of pictures for evidence *(Laugh.)* ...the look on their faces...HYSTERICAL!! ...and let me tell you...those big ole' ta-tas of hers are definitely...silicone city – look, I'll show ya'!

> (**LIZZY** *pulls out her cell phone and shows* **CAROLINE** *the photo.* **CAROLINE** *gasps.*)

BECCA. I was at home helpin' Rosie with her science fair project and here comes Lizzy runnin' in freakin' out and –

LIZZY. So, we called a locksmith...had all the locks changed and threw his clothes out on the driveway... and then we *set 'em on fire* –

BECCA. Not *WE* Lizzy...that fire part was *all* you –

LIZZY. ...and then I ran over them with the car...twice.

BECCA. *While* it was on fire. The fire department came out and everything. It was so embarrassin' –

> (**LIZZY** *laughs.* **BECCA** *looks uneasily at* **CAROLINE** *to indicate that* **LIZZY** *is unbalanced.*)

CAROLINE. I'm so sorry Becca...this must be awful for you.

BECCA. I'll be –

LIZZY. She'll be fine –

CAROLINE. *(Uneasy.)* Well...good then. So, how are the kids doin' with all this...how old are they now anyway?

BECCA. I've got pictures –

> (**BECCA** *pulls out her cellphone to show pictures.*)

They seem to be doin' okay...they don't know *everything* yet. Tucker was never home much anyway...this is Rose...she's fourteen, Daisy just turned twelve, Poppy is nine and Lily will be seven...next month.

CAROLINE. Lord have mercy...four girls.

BECCA. Soon to be five.

LIZZY. I told her she needs to name this one Ragweed or Kudzu.

BECCA. Stop it Lizzy. *(Then.)* I like flower names...and this precious girl is gonna be my Magnolia. *(She touches her tummy.)* Woo-wee... I am pooped.

LIZZY. Becca come over here and sit down. Caroline and I are makin' a list of things to do...we've gotta get Miss Polly's house packed up.

BECCA. Packed up?

CAROLINE. Yes, Chelsea and –

LIZZY. Chelsea and Michael want to sell it and they left it *all* for Caroline to do...they are just worthless...so *obviously*, I said I would help her...and we started a list –

(LIZZY begins throwing things in the trash.)

CAROLINE. Slow down Lizzy... I would like to see what you're throwin' out.

LIZZY. *(Ignoring.)* It's just trash sweetie...don't worry.

BECCA. Well let me help... I can make the list...give me that pad and pen –

CAROLINE. Oh Becca...you don't need to do that.

BECCA. I want to! Momma has the girls all week for Spring Break...and I need to do somethin' to keep my mind off plottin' my Texas chainsaw revenge on Tucker. Besides...it'll be fun catchin' up...it's been a hundred years –

(**LIZZY** *grabs the pad and pen for* **BECCA**.)

CAROLINE. Well...thank you Becca...that is really sweet of you –

LIZZY. *(Taking over.)* OK Becca...write down...boxes, tape, and big black magic markers...oh and bubble wrap. We can use some of these old newspapers for wrappin' fragile stuff too. Then we need to call down to the church thrift shop and ask Delford if we can use their van...or see if they will pick stuff up *(Beat.)* Then we need to decide if we are going to have a yard sale... OH ...and we need wine...*lots* of wine.

CAROLINE. Wine?

LIZZY. You don't think I can get through all this without a little buzz do ya?

CAROLINE. Well –

BECCA. I was over to the Piggy Wiggly yesterday and they had that boxed wine for buy two and get one free.

LIZZY. Perfect...put it on the list –

BECCA. *(Reading list.)* OK I have boxes, tape and markers on the list...bubble wrap...call Delford at the church and get a van...and wine...what else?

LIZZY. That's all for now I guess. Can you call the church Becca? Caroline...you start bringin' out more stuff and we'll go through it and put it in the carport –

CAROLINE. Lizzy...you are gonna need to slow down... this is all happenin' too fast...and I don't want to seem ungrateful...but you're gettin' a little like –

(Immediate tension.)

LIZZY. A little like *what*?

CAROLINE. *(Gingerly.)* You know how you get –

LIZZY. How I get?

CAROLINE. Nevermind, I shouldn't have said anything Lizzy... I'm just tired.

LIZZY. But tell me what you meant Caroline.

(CAROLINE and LIZZY stare at one another.)

BECCA. Lizzy...just let it go...okay?

LIZZY. *(Uppity.)* Well... I was wonderin' how long this was gonna take.

(BECCA dials the phone.)

CAROLINE. What?

LIZZY. You gettin' all up on your high horse...treatin' me like you're better than me –

CAROLINE. My high horse? *(Flustered.)* What are you... I am not –

LIZZY. Oh, please Caroline...don't try to act innocent.

CAROLINE. Lizzy...just forget it and go home –

BECCA. *(Loudly into phone.)* Hey there Delford...this is Becca Bailey...yeah...uh huh...any day now I hope... anyway... I had a couple of questions for ya'...but somethin' tells me I should probably just come over *there* instead. See ya' in a few sweetie...bye bye.

(BECCA waddles to the

door.)

LIZZY. What is your problem Caroline?

CAROLINE. My problem? *(Beat.)* *Really* Lizzy? *(Beat.)* Oh, I don't know...let me think...maybe I might be a little upset... SINCE MY MOMMA JUST DIED!

BECCA. *(Calm escape.)* OK then... I think little Magnolia and I will just toodle on over to the church and let you girls have a minute to sort this out. OK?

*(They ignore her and stare angrily at each other. **BECCA** grabs her purse and crosses to the door. She begins to exit and turns back.)*

BECCA. Don't forget...the emergency number is *nine-one-one*. K? Bye!

*(**BECCA**, a good Catholic, crosses herself and exits.)*

CAROLINE. LIZZY! I don't wanna get into *anything* with you...this is not the time to be hashin' up any old high school drama...please...just leave –

LIZZY. High school drama? Really?! You never even –

*(There is a quick knock at the door. **DONNA JO MARTIN** enters. She is dressed head to toe as the classic Dorothy of Oz. She carries a purse. She cannot see well without her glasses...but is too vain to wear them.)*

DONNA JO. Hello...yoo hoo...Caroline? Lizzy?

CAROLINE. Donna Jo?

*(**DONNA JO** crosses and pulls **LIZZY** to her and hugs her dramatically.)*

DONNA JO. Oh Caroline... I am so sorry to hear about Miss Polly.

LIZZY. I'm Lizzy...put your glasses on ya' dingbat.

*(**DONNA JO** squints at **LIZZY**...gets her glasses from her purse and puts them on...then grabs **CAROLINE** and dramatically hugs her.)*

DONNA JO. Oh Caroline... I am so sorry. We were right in the middle of a dress rehearsal when Lizzy called...but of course... I rushed right over.

CAROLINE. Well thank you Donna Jo...that is so sweet of you –

    (**DONNA JO** *pulls* **CAROLINE** *to her again dramatically.*)

DONNA JO. OH Caroline...you must be a mess... I can't even imagine –

CAROLINE. Yes, well I'm –

LIZZY. *(Still on edge.)* Donna Jo...what in God's name are you wearin'?

DONNA JO. *(Duh.)* My costume *(Beat.)* for the show... I just told the rest of the cast that I had to take a ten... and then I jumped in the car... I've got to go right back to finish up dress rehearsal...the Munchkins will be restless...we open in a week.

CAROLINE. So *(Beat.) you're* playin' the part of...Dorothy?

DONNA JO. Of course –

LIZZY. Well...when you said y'all were doing *The Wizard of Oz*... I thought you might be playin' the Auntie or maybe...um...the Witch... I mean...it seems like those would be...um...more *appropriate* parts...for someone your –

DONNA JO. What are you sayin' Lizzy?

CAROLINE. *(Aside.)* Watch out sweetie...she's in a mood.

LIZZY. Well Donna Jo... I'm just *sayin'*...that you're a little long in the tooth to be playin' a sixteen-year-old farm girl from Kansas...but hey...no judgement.

DONNA JO. *(Indignant.)* Long in the tooth? Lizzy...the director cast me in the role...and I'm happy to give my public what they want.

LIZZY. Your *public*? It's *community* theatre Donna Jo... you're not in New York anymore –

CAROLINE. *(Aside.)* She has *totally* gone off the rails –

LIZZY. You have lorded that *ONE, Off-Off-Broadway* show you did a million years ago, over everybody down at Petula Little Theatre. They all know there will be hell to pay if you don't get the leadin' role.

CAROLINE. Lizzy stop it.

DONNA JO. Elizabeth…who peed in your Wheaties this mornin'?

LIZZY. Excuse me? Oh no you didn't!

DONNA JO. Oh yes I did!

LIZZY. Oh no you –

CAROLINE. GIRLS! Um… I hate to interrupt this little love fest that you're havin' right here in the middle of my momma's livin' room…my momma that just *died* two days ago…but… I am mentally *and* physically exhausted…so if y'all don't mind… I think I will just go and take a nap. Maybe y'all could… I don't know… leave. Thanks. So much.

LIZZY. Now look what you have done Donna Jo…you are always causin' problems.

DONNA JO. *ME?*

LIZZY. So you really don't want my help?

CAROLINE. *(Appalled.)* Seriously? I can't believe – *(Calming beat.)* You know what? Right now, I just need to take a nap. I can't even think straight.

DONNA JO. Caroline sugar…you'll be in my prayers. Elizabeth…c'mon let's go and let her rest…you can come down to the theatre and watch the rest of dress rehearsal.

LIZZY. *(Aside.)* I'd rather eat glass –

> (**DONNA JO** *sticks out her tongue at* **LIZZY** *then hugs* **CAROLINE**.)

DONNA JO. Love you sweet friend...call me if you need me. *(She exits, singing.*)*

LIZZY. Bless her heart...she thinks she's Meryl Streep.

DONNA JO. *(Offstage.)* I heard that...bee-otch!

LIZZY. Look Caroline... I don't want us to argue.

CAROLINE. Lizzy... I –

LIZZY. I'm sorry if I was bein' – *(Beat.)* Look...let's start over... OK?

> *(**CAROLINE** looks at **LIZZY** with resigned hesitation.)*

CAROLINE. OK...sure Lizzy...but first I need a nap. I am exhausted...so let's just –

> *(**LIZZY** becomes a whirlwind. **CAROLINE** has no time to respond.)*

LIZZY. Of course, you are sweetie. *(Looks at watch.)* Well... it's about four thirty...so you go get your nap...and I'll call the girls and find out when they can get back over here. There is just so much to do... *(Beat.)* OH, I KNOW...we'll have a SLUMBER PARTY tonight... just like back in High School... OOOOO I could just tinkle. OK...so I'll go get the boxes...and tell the girls to be back here at...say six thirty – seven-ish? OK YAY...and don't worry... I'll bring plenty of wine...okay sweetie...see ya' later...get a good nap...bye now.

> *(**LIZZY** grabs her purse and exits.)*

CAROLINE. What? Lizzy...LIZZY!

---

*A license to produce *Packing Up Polly* does not include a performance license for any third-party or copyrighted music. Licensees should create an original composition or use music in the public domain. For further information, please see the Music and Third-Party Materials Use Note on page iii.

*(**CAROLINE** runs to the door, but **LIZZY** is gone.)*

CAROLINE. Wait...what just happened...did she say slumber party?

*(**CAROLINE** yells out the door.)* ARE YOU FRIGGIN' KIDDIN' ME?

*(**CAROLINE** closes the door and then crosses to the sofa and sits, picking up the box of ashes.)*

Well Momma...it looks like you're gonna get that wish. It looks like we're gonna be reconnectin'...whether I'm ready or not. *(**CAROLINE** fakes a smile and waves her hands in the air.)* YAAAAAAY!

Scene Two

(Later that evening. A high-spirited, contemporary 1970s gospel song featuring a female singer plays on the stereo. A framed photo of a "beehived" Miss Polly sits on the end of the stereo console with the box of ashes and a burning candle. The sofa is folded out into a bed. There are sleeping bags, pillows, and blankets piled around. There are still many open and stacked boxes sitting around the room. **DONNA JO**, wearing leopard pajamas, dances by the stove, lip-syncing into a spatula. **BECCA**, wearing a worn-out maternity gown and mismatched socks, reclines on the sofa bed. She has the elastic cap to a vintage portable hair dryer on her head. The dryer is on. She is holding a record album sleeve. **LIZZY** stands by the stereo console tapping her foot and banging a tambourine. She is wearing pink-striped pajamas and Miss Polly's beehive wig. A Styrofoam wig head is nearby. There is a box of wine on the coffee table. **LIZZY** lowers the music volume slightly as **DONNA JO** takes cookies from the oven.)*

BECCA. *(Loud.)* OOOOOOO I always loved this one. Miss Polly sure had a beautiful voice.

DONNA JO. *(Loud.)* She could really raise the roof and get people up on their feet.

LIZZY. *(Really loud.)* This was my favorite album she did with the PRAISE HIS NAME SINGERS.

---

* A license to produce *Packing up Polly* does not include a performance license for any third-party or copyrighted music. Licensees should create an original composition or use music in the public domain. For further information, please see the Music and Third-Party Materials Use Note on page iii.

> (**BECCA** *takes a picture of* **LIZZY** *on her cellphone using the flash.*)

LIZZY. *(Loud.)* Which album is this?

> (**BECCA** *turns around the album cover. The cover features a middle-aged woman wearing the same wig* **LIZZY** *is wearing and the title "The Higher The Hair, The Closer To God."*)

BECCA. *(Loudly.)* This album is *"The Higher the Hair, The Closer to God."* They released this one in 1978. WOO WEE sing it Miss Polly!

DONNA JO. *(Loud.)* Miss Polly sure did love her some big hair.

BECCA. WHAT?

LIZZY. Why are you yellin' Becca?

BECCA. WHAT?

> (**LIZZY** *turns off the record.*)

DONNA JO. Turn that thing off!

BECCA. WHAT?

> (**LIZZY** *crosses over and pulls the cap off her head and turns off the dryer*)

LIZZY. Why are you wearin' that thing?

BECCA. Ya' old stick in the mud…it's just for fun! Don't you remember when we used to come over here the night before the football games? We would all take turns rollin' up our hair and gettin' under this dryer so we could have our big game day hair?

DONNA JO. Oh yes…and Miss Polly would tease and spray us within an inch of our lives…and then make us fried bologna and minna' cheese sammiches… OH…and remember those big ole white hairbows we used to wear? They were *huge*.

LIZZY. I loved those big ole bows...and my big hair –

BECCA. I miss those days...when we were all together... and best friends.

> (**CAROLINE** *enters in her pajamas. She is carrying a box with the words "Caroline's Room" written on it.*)

CAROLINE. Why are y'all out here yellin'? The neighbors are gonna call the police! *(Beat.)* Lizzy...why are you wearin' my momma's wig?

LIZZY. Oh...uh... I found it in Miss Polly's closet. I really think I can pull it off...this could be a whole new look for me. What do you think girls?

CAROLINE. *(Stern.)* Please, take that *off* Lizzy.

> (**LIZZY** *takes off the wig.*)

Give me that!

> (**CAROLINE** *sits the box down and takes the wig from* **LIZZY**. *She puts it on the Styrofoam head.*)

LIZZY. I didn't mean to upset you.

CAROLINE. I'm not upset Elizabeth...you just look ridiculous...and I didn't want to laugh at you.

> (*Everyone laughs, relieved.*)

BECCA. Don't worry girls, I have photographic proof for blackmail later... I'll text 'em to y'all.

> (**CAROLINE** *takes the album from* **BECCA** *and looks at the back.*)

CAROLINE. Momma sure did have a beautiful voice –

LIZZY. This was my favorite album.

CAROLINE. My favorite song has always been *"Kickin' Up My Heels For Jesus."*

BECCA. Oh yes... I love that one! You used to sing it with her onstage when you were little, didn't you Caroline?

CAROLINE. Yes. I loved singin' with Momma.

DONNA JO. I just loved it when Miss Polly would get to bangin' on that tambourine and stompin' that foot.

BECCA. And the next thing ya' knew...she was *twirlin'* cartwheels across the stage.

LIZZY. I don't know how she kept that wig on her head.

CAROLINE. Oh, *I do*...duct tape, thirty-two bobby pins... and a prayer.

BECCA. Well...what's in that box Caroline?

CAROLINE. I don't know...it says Caroline's room... probably just some of my old clothes –

DONNA JO. I'm hungry. What do you have to eat that pairs well with boxed White Zinfandel?

LIZZY. There's a little bit of that macaroni and cheese left I think –

BECCA. No, Magnolia and I already polished that off –

(**LIZZY** *crosses to the kitchen table and looks in a container.*)

CAROLINE. I know there's a whole bunch of Kentucky fried chicken in the fridge.

DONNA JO. Well, let me get some before Becca eats it all.

(**DONNA JO** *crosses to the refrigerator.*)

BECCA. Hey, bring me a leg and don't judge me... I'm eatin' for two.

LIZZY. Two *hundred*?

BECCA. Shut up or I'll eat *your* leg Lizzy.

> (**DONNA JO** *grabs a KFC bucket* from the refrigerator and crosses back to* **BECCA**. **CAROLINE** *opens the "Caroline's Room" box and pulls out a couple of trophies, a stuffed animal, and an extra-large set of cheerleader pom poms.*)

CAROLINE. I can't believe Momma saved all this.

> (**LIZZY** *looks in the box and pulls out a framed picture.*)

LIZZY. Look girls...this picture was taken at our very last homecomin' game.

> *(They gather around the picture.)*

BECCA. Let me see. *(Scowl.)* God, I was skinny then...look at my teensy little butt.

DONNA JO. There's not a single stitch of cellulite on my thighs.

CAROLINE. Those were the days –

> (**LIZZY** *grabs the photo.*)

LIZZY. Look at me... I AM GORGEOUS! *(Aside.)* But... I mean...really... I basically still look the same.

> *(Everyone rolls their eyes.* **LIZZY** *turns to* **BECCA** *and* **DONNA JO** *expecting compliments.)*

BECCA.	**DONNA JO.**
Oh...yeah...you look great...	You haven't changed a bit.

---

* A license to produce *Packing Up Polly* does not include a license to publicly display any branded logos or trademarked images. Licensees must acquire rights for any logos and/or images or create their own.

*(**LIZZY** pulls an overly large white hair bow out of the box and clips it on top of her head. She finds a small cheer megaphone and uses it to speak.)*

LIZZY. Hey girls I know...let's do a cheer.

BECCA. *(Snort laugh.)* Seriously?

CAROLINE. Um... I don't think so.

LIZZY. C'mon...it'll be fun.

*(**LIZZY** crosses left, takes a cheer stance, and looks expectantly at the **GIRLS**.)*

CAROLINE. I'll pass –

DONNA JO. I don't have enough of a buzz yet... I need more wine –

BECCA. Not me...little Magnolia is finally takin' a nap. I think we'll just sit here and make a video to put up on Facebook.

LIZZY. It'll be fun. Do y'all remember the pork chop cheer? Let's do it...c'mon –

*(**LIZZY** stomps her foot and gives **BECCA** a look.)*

DONNA JO. *(Taking a bite of chicken.)* OK fine... I'll do it...but only 'cause I know you won't shut up 'til I do.

LIZZY. Yep –

BECCA. OK fine... Wake up my little Magnolia blossom. She may as well start learnin' now... I plan to put her on a squad as soon as she can walk.

CAROLINE. Are all your girls cheerin' Becca?

BECCA. *(Duh.)* Of course, they are.

DONNA JO. Oh Caroline...remember when we said we were gonna open a cheerleadin' school?

CAROLINE. *(Fondly.)* Yes... I always wanted to do that –

BECCA. Actually, I think it was gonna be a cheerleadin' and dance school –

DONNA JO. And a baton twirlin'.

BECCA. ...and beauty pageant trainin'...right?

CAROLINE. *(Distant.)* Yes...yes it was –

DONNA JO. That would have been so fun... I wish we had –

LIZZY. *(Goading.)* We couldn't since she blew us off and skipped town.

DONNA JO.	**BECCA.**
Dammit Lizzy!	Lizzy!

CAROLINE. Ya' know...for someone who said to me this mornin' "Let's let bygones be bygones" –

*(**BECCA** sensing tension, breaks in.)*

BECCA. C'mon girls...let's do the cheer. I'm up...little Magnolia's up...now get me some DING-DANG POM POMS!

DONNA JO. *(Sarcastic.)* Yes...fun...can't wait...

LIZZY. Fine...whatever –

*(**DONNA JO** gives **BECCA** the pom poms from the box and they line up with **LIZZY**. They all look at **CAROLINE** expectantly.)*

CAROLINE. Oh, I see... *I'm* the party pooper if I don't do a cheer with y'all and make a big ole fool of myself.

BECCA, DONNA JO & LIZZY. YES!

CAROLINE. This is ridiculous –

*(**CAROLINE** begrudgingly crosses to get in line. **CAROLINE** gives **LIZZY** a look and*

gesture that says, "You're in my Head Cheer spot," and they switch places.)

BECCA. OK Cheer Captain…let's do this.

(**CAROLINE** *rolls her eyes and huffs. They all take a pre-cheer stance.)*

CAROLINE. *(Half-hearted.)* OK Tiger Ladies…pork chop cheer…ready? Okay.

(Everyone looks at **CAROLINE** *with disappointment.)*

LIZZY. How are we supposed to get fired up for the game with that piss poor attitude, Caroline?

DONNA JO. I mean…yeah…really –

CAROLINE. *(Irritated but loud.)* FINE! *(Beat.)* OK Tiger Ladies… PORK CHOP CHEER – READY? OK!

(They launch into a semi-together cheer from memory. The cheer involves a lot of arm movement, shimmies, and kicks. **BECCA** *is much more exuberant and louder than the others.)*

ALL. PORK CHOP PORK CHOP GREASY GREASY… WE CAN BEAT YOUR TEAM EASY EASY! PORK CHOP PORK CHOP GREASY GREASY… THE TIGERS WILL BEAT YOU EASY EASY! SHAKE IT TO THE LEFT… SHAKE IT TO THE RIGHT… SHAKE THAT TIGER SPIRIT WITH ALL YOUR MIGHT! WOO! GOOOOOOOOOOO TIGERS!

(They growl and hiss like cats, scratching at the air with their "fighting claws." **DONNA JO** *tries to do a kick and then grabs her back. An overly-exuberant* **BECCA** *continues with another cheer as the others stare…mouths agape.)*

BECCA. FIRECRACKER FIRECRACKER BOOM BOOM BOOM! FIRECRACKER FIRECRACKER BOOM BOOM BOOM! The boys got the muscles...the teachers got the brains...the girls got the pretty legs, and we won the game. WOO YEAH... GO TIGERS!!!

CAROLINE. OK Becca...that's enough.

(**BECCA** *continues cheering.*)

BECCA. U-G-L-Y... YOU AIN'T GOT NO ALIBI... YOU UGLY... HEY HEY... YOU UGLY!

LIZZY, CAROLINE & DONNA JO. BECCA!

BECCA. *(Pooping out.)* WOO YEAH!!!! GOOOOOOO TIGERS! TIGERS ALL THE WAY!!! YEAH!!! TOUCHDOWN!!!

DONNA JO. Lord have mercy...her water is gonna break and she is gonna go into labor right here.

BECCA. From your lips...to God's ear honey... I wish!

LIZZY. Becca *sit down* –

BECCA. Whew... Magnolia blossom and I are *definitely* ready for another chicken leg *now*.

(**BECCA** *crosses to get a piece of chicken.*)

DONNA JO. I can't eat another bite... I am as full as a tick.

CAROLINE. Well... I'm gonna go pull the rest of the stuff out of my closet –

LIZZY. *THEN* we get to start on the attic –

BECCA. ...and the storage shed –

LIZZY. Don't forget the two storage units over in Petula.

DONNA JO. Two storage units? Really?

CAROLINE. *(Quietly embarrassed.)* Actually, it's three.

LIZZY. Oh...that's right...three.

BECCA. *(Eating.)* Lordy mercy... Miss Polly was a *big-time* hoarder...like on that TV show.

LIZZY. *(Shushing.)* Caroline doesn't like that word.

CAROLINE. *(Sad.)* No...it's not that...it's just...I feel like all this stuff meant more to Momma than me. I asked her to move up to Atlanta...but when I suggested cleaning things out...throwing stuff out...she got *really* angry with me...and threw a tee-total hissy fit. She didn't speak to me for weeks.

DONNA JO. It's a psychological disorder...they can't help it... there's even a TV show about it now.

    (**CAROLINE** *crosses to the bedrooms.*)

    (**DONNA JO** *and* **BECCA** *exchange an uncomfortable look.*)

LIZZY. Want some help in there?

CAROLINE. No... I need a minute to myself...please.

    (**CAROLINE** *exits.*)

DONNA JO. Bless her heart... I don't know how she's gettin' through all this.

BECCA. That's why we're here. *(Then.)* Uh...well...the carport is almost full to the ceilin'. What time is the church van comin' to get the first load?

DONNA JO. Between eight and nine in the mornin' –

    (**LIZZY** *checks that* **CAROLINE** *is gone.*)

LIZZY. *(Low tone.)* Hey...don't y'all think it's a little weird that Patrick didn't come with Caroline?

BECCA. Well, I wasn't gonna say anything...but yeah... I do –

DONNA JO. Lizzy…don't start stirrin' the pot tonight. *(Beat.)* But I mean…yeah I do –

LIZZY. She told *me*…that he is at some important meetin' he couldn't miss.

DONNA JO. Oh…c'mon…you just don't…*not* show up for your mother-in-law's funeral.

BECCA. Do y'all think they're havin' problems?

LIZZY. Miss Polly told me their marriage is perfect…like a fairy tale.

BECCA. Perfect? B.S! There's no such thing! Every marriage is just one big-busted bimbo away from disaster!

DONNA JO. Don't I know it –

BECCA. Oh, I'm sorry… I forgot –

DONNA JO. Forgot what…that I have lost in love…nine times?

BECCA. *Nine* times?

LIZZY. Everyone always forgets Bunky –

BECCA. Oh *yeah*… Bunky –

LIZZY. I *still* can't believe you married a carny.

DONNA JO. *(Dreamy.)* Bunky Thornton…mm mm mm. What can I say? He looked *real* good in that sweaty tank top and those skin-tight Levis. *(Beat.)* I don't know…maybe I was still dizzy from the tilt-a-whirl… but that was three of the best days of my life –

BECCA. Y'all were only married for three days?

DONNA JO. *(Distant look.)* Yeah…he said a carny can't be tied down to one place…they need the freedom of the open road and…the *thrill* of the midway.

BECCA. Well...on the bright side...you only need one more punch in your Frequent Bride Rewards Card...and your next weddin' will be free.

LIZZY. Well... I wouldn't know anything about that sort of thing... Bobby and I have a wonderful marriage. He lets me travel all over the state with my Miss Georgia Belle pageants...and more importantly...he knows that if he looks at or *even thinks* about another woman... I will suffocate him in his sleep. It's a perfect marriage.

> (**LIZZY** *crosses to the kitchen, oblivious of the death stares.*)

BECCA.	**DONNA JO.**
(Snide.) Good for you!	*(Snide.)* Well, lucky you –

> (**CAROLINE** *reenters holding an old scrapbook. It is decorated with stickers and glitter. It is overfilled with pictures, clippings, and mementoes.*)

CAROLINE. Girls...y'all are not gonna believe this... look what I found in the closet...our old Cheer Club scrapbook. You should see some of these pictures.

DONNA JO.	**BECCA.**	**LIZZY.**
Really?	Shut up –	Let me see that.

> (*They gather around the scrapbook.* **BECCA** *gnaws on a chicken leg.*)

DONNA JO. OH NO...look at this...this is when Momma made me get that awful spiral perm...and y'all tried to comb it out.

CAROLINE. You poor thing –

BECCA. You look like you were electrocuted...like you were pardoned about thirty seconds after they threw the switch.

(They laugh. **LIZZY** *spots another photo.)*

LIZZY. Oh my word…look at this… I think this is Junior Prom…

(**LIZZY** *pulls the photo out of the scrapbook.* **BECCA** *takes it.)*

BECCA. *(Disgust.)* I look like I'm wearin' a ruffled potato sack.

LIZZY. Is it burlap?

(**DONNA JO** *takes the picture.)*

DONNA JO. Now *that*…is one ugly dress.

BECCA. Don't y'all remember? Momma insisted that I was covered from head to toe.

DONNA JO. Oh yeah –

LIZZY, DONNA JO & CAROLINE. *(Singsong.)* "Good girls don't show their bosom cleavage Rebecca Ann."

CAROLINE. Now… Donna Jo on the other hand…looks like she took the night off from workin' her street corner to come to prom.

DONNA JO. *(Gasp.)* I do! *(Beat.)* Why did I even bother wearin' a top?

CAROLINE. If I remember correctly…you didn't wear it very long. Didn't we find you in Jimmy Don Ledford's backseat that night?

DONNA JO. *(Giggles.)* Don't judge me… I married him didn't I?

LIZZY. YES! Marriage number one…of many –

BECCA. *(Sweetly.)* Look Caroline…you're wearin' your Homecoming crown in this picture –

CAROLINE. *(Distant.)* Uh huh… I see that –

(LIZZY's mood takes a turn.)

LIZZY. *(Sassy.)* Homecomin' Queen, Head Cheerleader *and* Prom Queen... *OH* and President of our class. *(Snotty.)* Senior year was just *super* great for you... wasn't it Caroline? I wish I knew what it's like to be *perfect*...don't you girls?

BECCA. *(Uneasy.)* Oh no...wait...what's happenin'? What's happenin' right now?

(Uncomfortable moment of silence.)

DONNA JO. *(Peacemaker.)* Weeelllll...what else is in there Becca? Oh look...what's that?

BECCA. I think it's movie tickets Donna Jo –

DONNA JO. *(Loud.)* Yes! Oh wow...look...y'all remember this? This is when we all snuck out to see *Risky Business* at the old Plaza Twin Drive-In.

BECCA. *(Gasps.)* YES... Momma would have killed me deader than a doornail if she had found out I watched Tom Cruise dancin' around in his underwear.

DONNA JO. *(Forced laugh.)* ...and remember... I didn't have enough money to get in...so y'all put me in the trunk of the car...and –

BECCA. THAT'S RIGHT!! We forgot you were in there... and ran off to the concession stand –

DONNA JO. I was in there for a half hour bangin' and yellin' for help...and then I peed on myself.

BECCA. And then we couldn't find Lizzy to get the keys and let you out –

(They giggle uncomfortably and continue flipping pages.)

LIZZY. *(Goading.)* Caroline...that's the night Patrick first asked you out...isn't it?

(Beat.)

CAROLINE. *(Rattled.)* Um...was it? I don't –

BECCA. *(Oblivious.)* And then they got married...and we all wore those big –

LIZZY. WOOP-TEE-DOO! Caroline married the star quarterback and rode off into the sunset wearin' a rhinestone tiara...just another *super* awesome day in her *super* perfect life!

(Another uncomfortable silence falls over the room.)

BECCA. Weeelllll y'all...let's see what else is in here. Look... here's our first –

LIZZY. Oh, shut up Rebecca...you too Donna Jo –

DONNA JO. Excuse me? Did someone forget their medication today?

*(**LIZZY** stomps off to the kitchen table. **CAROLINE** follows.)*

CAROLINE. This is insanity Lizzy... I knew I should have told you no, when you offered to help. What was I thinkin'?

*(**CAROLINE** begins to cry and exits to the bedrooms. **LIZZY** yells to her.)*

LIZZY. Yeah...that's just great Caroline...run away and desert us...like you always do!

DONNA JO. Well...this is shapin' up to be a *super* fun night.

BECCA. It's certainly the best "pack up your long lost high school friend's recently deceased mother's hoarder house slumber party" I've ever been to. Thanks *Elizabeth*.

DONNA JO. You need some therapy Lizzy...*serious* therapy!

*(**BECCA** and **DONNA JO** glare at **LIZZY**.)*

LIZZY. We made a lot of plans together...that cheerleadin' school was *our* dream...and Miss Perfect...just up and leaves town...don't try and act like you're both not as angry as I am.

BECCA. I am *not* angry...but even if I were... I would certainly choose a more appropriate time to air my grievances...

DONNA JO. I mean really Lizzy...it's been over twenty years honey...let it go honey... Let. It. Go. Pick up the pieces and *move on* with your life!

LIZZY. I can't let it go...she took our dreams and threw them away –

BECCA. No ma'am... I got my dream *(Beat.)* well...up until my husband cheated on me with a pre-teen bimbo... but I *got* my dream. My dream was always to be a wife and mother –

LIZZY. Oh please... I remember how upset you were. You cried and cried for days. We made a pact that we would be together...forever.

BECCA. I was seventeen-years-old Lizzy...*everything* devastated me back then.

DONNA JO. Lizzy if you let that one moment in time, shape the course of your whole life...then you have only yourself to blame.

LIZZY. *(Grasping.)* ...and you Donna Jo...you...you –

DONNA JO. *(Putting her hand up.)* Stop it E-lizabeth... don't go there... I took my dreams and went to New York...and nothin' you can say will *ever* take that away from me...and if you make one snide...condescending comment...I swear I'll –

(**CAROLINE** *reenters and crosses to* **LIZZY**.)

BECCA.	**DONNA JO.**
Uh-oh	Oh hell –

CAROLINE. *(Distraught.)* I *cannot* believe I have let you come in here and do this to me. I should have known you'd dredge up the past.

> (**CAROLINE** *exits and then immediately returns.*)

OK Lizzy... I get it... I do...and I'm sorry that things didn't work out like we all planned. *(Beat.)* but...there are things that you don't even know about...and... I didn't want to... I mean... I tried Lizzy...but –

LIZZY. You *tried*? What do you mean you *tried*? Seems to me the only thing you *tried*...was to disappear. *(Beat.)* Oh Caroline, you're such a saint! *(Beat.)* I KNOW... I KNOW Y'ALL...we should have a *"She tried"* parade... for Saint Caroline of Savannah.

> (**CAROLINE** *storms out.*)

DONNA JO. OK that's it...time to go Lizzy.

LIZZY. Go? Go where?

> (**CAROLINE** *calls from offstage.*)

CAROLINE. I KNOW WHERE YOU CAN GO!

BECCA. Maybe Donna Jo's right Lizzy –

LIZZY. *(Grasping.)* Well... I don't have my car...remember? Donna Jo picked me up.

DONNA JO. Oh yeah...that's right...okay...let's go... I'm takin' you home.

> (**DONNA JO** *grabs her purse and crosses to the front door.*)

LIZZY. I don't wanna go home...I'm not finished.

DONNA JO. Oh yes you are missy.

BECCA. Y'all aren't leavin' me here are you?

DONNA JO. Don't worry... I'll come back after I drop Lizzy off AT THE CLOSEST ASYLUM!!

BECCA. Are you just gonna leave in your pajamas?

CAROLINE. *(Offstage.)* What is wrong with you Lizzy? You are the devil... THE DEVIL!!!!

BECCA. OK ...yeah...go...you're leavin' in your pajamas... go...right now.

DONNA JO. Yep...that's your cue Lizzy...get your purse... let's hit it.

LIZZY. Don't worry Caroline... THE *DEVIL* IS LEAVIN'!

BECCA. Stop it!

> (**CAROLINE** *steps into the doorway.*)

CAROLINE. GOOD! Don't let the door hit ya...where the good Lord split ya!

> (**CAROLINE** *exits.*)

DONNA JO. *LET'S GO* Lizzy!

> (**DONNA JO** *pulls* **LIZZY** *to the door.* **LIZZY** *grabs for the box of wine.* **DONNA JO** *smacks her hand.*)

No ma'am... I don't think so. Leave the wine... *LEAVE THE WINE* –

> (**LIZZY** *and* **DONNA JO** *exit.* **BECCA** *grabs her purse and steps in the hallway door.*)

BECCA. I'm just gonna go with them hon, and give you a minute...to...decompress or whatever...but...maybe we'll run by the Burger Barn for a banana cream pie milkshake...you want me to bring you one?

CAROLINE. *(Offstage.)* NO!

> (**BECCA** *exits. A few seconds later,* **CAROLINE** *returns. She crosses center and looks up.*)

CAROLINE. WELL, THANK YOU MOMMA! THIS IS SUPER FUN! *(Beat.)* I don't remember when I've had such a good time! What's next? A PLAGUE OF LOCUSTS?

> *(**BECCA** returns in a hurry. She is startled to see **CAROLINE**.)*

BECCA. Oh...hey sweetie...sorry... I'm just grabbin' a leg for the road... *(Beat.)* and um...a thigh...and um –

> *(A car horn honks. **BECCA** grabs the entire bucket of chicken and a roll of paper towels and quickly exits gnawing on a chicken leg. **CAROLINE** crosses to the stereo and turns on the record again...turning the volume down low.* She takes Polly's ashes, then crosses to the sofa and sits. She suddenly lets out a loud scream.)*

CAROLINE. OK MOMMA...WHERE DID YOU HIDE THE VALIUM?

> *(Blackout.)*

End of Act One

---

* A license to produce *Packing Up Polly* does not include a performance license for any third-party or copyrighted music. Licensees should create an original composition or use music in the public domain. For further information, please see the Music and Third-Party Materials Use Note on page iii.

ACT TWO

Scene One

(Four days later. The room is almost completely bare. The walls are bare. The curtains are down. The sofa, coffee table, and kitchen table are the only furniture that remain. There are a few donation boxes stacked near the front door labeled with their destinations. A blender sits on the kitchen table with a bottle of tequila and red party cups. Miss Polly's ashes, now in a pretty urn, and the scrapbook are on the coffee table. A peppy gospel song plays on the stereo.* There is a box on top of the stereo console labeled CAROLINE'S DO NOT DONATE. **CAROLINE** *enters carrying a trophy and a stuffed animal. She crosses and puts them in the box...then turns off the record and puts it in the record sleeve.* **DONNA JO** *enters through the front door. She has a clipboard and pen.)*

DONNA JO. OK sweetie...the van is packed...and Delford is taking it all on back over to the church. He said they'll be back tomorrow mornin' for the last of the big pieces.

---

* A license to produce *Packing Up Polly* does not include a performance license for any third-party or copyrighted music. Licensees should create an original composition or use music in the public domain. For further information, please see the Music and Third-Party Materials Use Note on page iii.

CAROLINE. Thanks Donna Jo.

DONNA JO. *(Flirty smile.)* And...that real estate agent is supposed to be here this afternoon around four. *(Flirty smile.)* Don't worry... I'll handle him.

CAROLINE. Okay...thanks.

DONNA JO. Have you heard from Chelsea or Michael?

CAROLINE. No. *(Beat.)* Well...there *was* a call last night... but I think it was a butt dial... I could hear slot machines chingin' in the background.

DONNA JO. *(Laugh.)* So...it could have been either one of them.

> (**CAROLINE** *lowers her head into her hands.* **DONNA JO** *sits beside her.)*

CAROLINE. Yeah –

DONNA JO. Bless your heart...you are just worn to a frazzle aren't you?

CAROLINE. I haven't slept much. Everything happened so fast...Momma just died six days ago...and now... everything she owned and cherished her whole life, has been picked through, plundered, and discarded...and all I have left is this box...and a few of her records.

DONNA JO. And the memories Caroline –

CAROLINE. Yes, the memories.

DONNA JO. I know this is hard darlin'...but I don't think Miss Polly really *cherished* all this stuff. I think she just had...a little problem. You know she didn't love all this stuff...more than you.

CAROLINE. Thank you Donna Jo... I need to believe that –

> *(We hear a toilet flush.* **BECCA** *waddles in from the hallway. She is more "together" now, wearing makeup, styled hair and a pretty maternity dress. She carries a stack of old towels.)*

BECCA. I swear, Magnolia is tap dancin' on my bladder... wearin' little baby cha-cha pumps. *(Beat.)* By the way...there's still a few more things in the back of the bathroom closet.

> (**BECCA** *places the towels on the stereo console.*)

CAROLINE. Becca Bailey...get your fanny over here and sit down...you are doin' too much.

BECCA. DUH! I'm tryin' to go into labor Caroline. Want me to rotate your tires? Do you have any wood I could chop?

> (**BECCA** *does a few rapid Lamaze breaths and squats.*)

DONNA JO. *(Laughing.)* OMG...that reminds me of this story I heard on the radio this mornin'...on NPR –

CAROLINE. About a pregnant lady choppin' wood?

DONNA JO. Noooo...about this woman goin' into labor... it's hysterical.

BECCA. This ought to be good.

DONNA JO. Oh it is...it is...okay...so these women decided to have a big fancy baby shower for their friend...*but* they didn't know she had that crazy phobia thing where she is scared to death of clowns.

BECCA. Oh no –

DONNA JO. I mean...literally *terrified* of 'em...

CAROLINE. Coulrophobia.

BECCA. Cool-o what?

CAROLINE. *(Matter of fact.)* Coulrophobia...it's the intense and irrational fear of clowns.

> (**BECCA** *and* **DONNA JO** *stare blankly at* **CAROLINE** *for a beat.*)

DONNA JO. *(Whatever.)* Uh huh...anyway...they had this clown named Pooty...come ridin' in on a unicycle.

CAROLINE. Pooty...the clown?

DONNA JO. Yes! He comes ridin' in on a unicycle...honkin' his little clown horn...and the woman goes *completely* insane...screamin' and carryin' on...and *then* she picks up a baby stroller and starts swingin' it at Pooty... hits him right upside the head...and knocked him right off that unicycle.

BECCA.	**CAROLINE.**
Bless her heart.	That's hysterical –

DONNA JO. Wait, it gets better. In all the excitement...her water breaks and she goes into labor.

CAROLINE.	**BECCA.**
Nooooooooo –	Lucky girl

DONNA JO. But get this...*this* is the best part. You're gonna die! Pooty the clown was *actually* a paramedic...he just did the clown thing on the weekends for extra cash... so anyway...she ended up havin' her baby *delivered*...by Pooty the clown right there on the floor in front of all her friends...screamin' in terror...the whole time–

CAROLINE. *(Laughing.)* That poor woman –

BECCA. Well... SEND IN THE CLOWNS Y'ALL...because if I don't go into labor soon... I'm gonna start joggin' up and down Victory Drive.

DONNA JO. Oooo that would be attractive.

BECCA. There would be an all-points bulletin out for a joggin' whale on the loose...and then Green Peace would come and try to drag me back into the ocean.

CAROLINE. Stop it Rebecca...you're beautiful...you're just... uh...a little knocked up right now.

DONNA JO. Speakin' of beautiful...why are you all dolled up and wearin' makeup?

CAROLINE. You do look real nice Rebecca.

BECCA. Thanks...actually...if I'm being honest...I heard there's a hot new obstetrician at Savannah General... and well...since Doctor Dixon is laid up with a broken foot...and I'm gonna pop any second... I want to look cute when y'all wheel me in there... I just might get a hot date.

CAROLINE. He's not gonna be lookin' at your face darlin' –

DONNA JO. Talk about lookin' for love in all the wrong places.

*(**DONNA JO** picks up the scrapbook and flips the pages.)*

CAROLINE. So... I guess this means you have no desire to try and work things out with Tucker?

BECCA. ARE YOU SERIOUS? That will never happen. Tucker Bailey is dead to me. D – E – A – D! DEAD! *(Beat.)* Well...except for *after* the divorce...on his court-ordered weekends...when he will be getting the kids... while I date my hot new doctor boyfriend and *lover*. *(Switch.)* Otherwise... DEAD. TO. ME.

CAROLINE. Becca...your hormones have gone berserk.

*(**DONNA JO** pulls a photo out of the scrapbook.)*

DONNA JO. Look at this...oh my word...this is when we did the Junior Miss Savannah pageant.

CAROLINE. How old were we there?

DONNA JO. Fifteen or sixteen?

BECCA. *(Squints.)* Am I wearing baby's breath in my hair?

CAROLINE. Yes...yes you are.

DONNA JO. It looks like you have a bush growin' out of your head.

BECCA. Y'all know Momma made me wear it.

CAROLINE & DONNA JO. *(Singsong.)* "You look just like an angel from heaven Rebecca Ann."

BECCA. Y'all can kiss my big pregnant butt.

CAROLINE. Who is that with the big dyed, fried-out hair?

(They all look close at the photo.)

DONNA JO. That's Vivian Keiser.

BECCA. That's right...poor thing...her hair looks like cotton candy. *(Beat.)* What was it we used to call hair like that?

DONNA JO. SLUT FUZZ!

BECCA. *(Laughing.)* Yes... Slut Fuzz!!!

CAROLINE. Dyed

BECCA. Fried

CAROLINE, BECCA & DONNA JO. – And *laid* to the side.

(They giggle.)

BECCA. I thought Lizzy was in this pageant.

CAROLINE. She was...isn't she in the picture?

*(**CAROLINE** takes the photo.)*

DONNA JO. She was definitely in the pageant...we all were –

CAROLINE. I know she was...because she almost burnt down the Civic Center with her fire batons...and the fire department had to come out.

*(**BECCA** takes back the photo.)*

BECCA. *(Squints.)* Wait...there she is...behind you Caroline. You can hardly see her for that big hair of yours...and that enormous crown you're wearin'.

DONNA JO. *(Puzzled.)* She looks sad. *(Beat.)* Actually, she looks mad –

BECCA. Poor thing...she has always had that restin' bitch face.

(**BECCA** *pulls out another photo.*)

She looks upset in this one too.

(**DONNA JO** *pulls out a photo.*)

DONNA JO. This one too.

CAROLINE. Where are we in this one?

DONNA JO. I think it's the Miss Georgia Belle pageant... the picture is a little grainy though.

BECCA. *(Squints.)* Yes...yes it is...that's what is says on your sash Caroline... Miss Georgia Belle 1984. Now *that* is a big crown. Gosh you won a lot of crowns didn't you?

(**CAROLINE** *stares out blankly.*)

CAROLINE. But Lizzy never won –

DONNA JO. And now, Lizzy owns Miss Georgia Belle... isn't that funny?

(**CAROLINE** *throws her hands up.*)

CAROLINE. Well, it's no wonder Lizzy hates me –

BECCA. Oh...now Caroline...she doesn't hate you.

DONNA JO. *(Maybe she does.)* Weellllll –

CAROLINE. How could she not?

BECCA. She loves you Caroline –

DONNA JO. *(I don't think so.)* Weellllll –

(**CAROLINE** *takes the scrapbook and flips the pages.*)

CAROLINE. Look at this...and this...and *THIS*...every picture of me has a crown on my head or a first-place medal or big ole trophy...and then there's Lizzy standin' in the background. I'm sorry I was such an overachiever, girls... I just wanted Momma to be proud of me.

BECCA. What?

DONNA JO. Oh Caroline... Miss Polly was *always* proud of you.

(**CAROLINE** *turns away.*)

CAROLINE. Do you know she only came to one football game to see me cheer? It was that last game of our senior year...when we went to State. Six years of cheerleadin' and she only came to that one game –

BECCA. *(Gentle.)* But Caroline...she always had us come over to get ready...and make us fried bologna sandwiches...and rolled up our hair...remember? Then she had to go sing.

CAROLINE. I just...never felt like I could never live up to Chelsea and Michael...or her fans...or *(Sweeping gesture.)* all her...stuff. I've spent my entire life... competin' for my mother's attention.

BECCA. Caroline...that is *not* true –

(*There is a knock at the door. The door opens a little and an arm appears, waving a white cloth.*)

LIZZY. *(Yelling.)* PLEASE DON'T SHOOT Y'ALL... I COME IN PEACE –

(**LIZZY** *sticks her head in the door.* **DONNA JO** *crosses to stop her.*)

DONNA JO. EXCUSE ME!? NO MA'AM! I issued you a personal restrainin' order and told you not to come within a hundred yards of this house.

*(**CAROLINE** quickly exits right. **LIZZY** enters, still waving the flag. **DONNA JO** grabs the flag.)*

LIZZY. Well... I was just on my way to see Momma over in Petula...and I *happened* to be drivin' right by here and saw y'all's cars...so I –

DONNA JO. – decided to come by and cause more drama?

LIZZY. I want to see Caroline. Where is she?

*(**LIZZY** crosses toward the stage right doorway. **DONNA JO** stops her.)*

DONNA JO. *That* is definitely not a good idea.

LIZZY. *(Pulling away.)* Please... Donna Jo...please –

BECCA. *(Shocked.)* She said please –

DONNA JO. *(Gasp.)* She did –

*(**DONNA JO** checks **LIZZY** for a fever.)*

Are you okay? Are you sick? Are you dyin'?

LIZZY. *Not funny. (Beat.)* But I'm sure I deserve that.

DONNA JO. Yeah...you do. *(Resigned.)* OK...sit down... I'm gonna check on Caroline. *(Beat.)* But *don't* get comfortable...you may be leavin' right away –

*(**DONNA JO** exits. **BECCA** immediately jumps on **LIZZY**.)*

BECCA. What's wrong with you Lizzy? You have been completely *wacko* for the last six months.

LIZZY. *Wacko?* What are you talkin' about?

BECCA. *Really?* Let's see...hmmm...you are nasty to *literally everybody*...includin' me your best friend... you set all of Tucker's clothes on fire in my front yard and ran over 'em with your BMW while hangin' out the window screamin' *"DIE CHEATIN' PIG DIE – WOOP WOOP WOOP"* at the top of your lungs –

LIZZY. OK...but I did that for –

BECCA. – not to mention...you verbally attacked Caroline on the same day as Miss Polly's funeral...shall I go on?

>(**LIZZY** *is momentarily silenced and resigned.*)

LIZZY. Well...yeah...there is that.

BECCA. I mean... I'm a little scared of you right now darlin' –

>(**DONNA JO** *reenters.*)

DONNA JO. Me too –

LIZZY. *(Sincere.)* I'm *sorry* girls.

>(**LIZZY** *sits on the sofa.* **DONNA JO** *and* **BECCA** *sit either side of her.*)

DONNA JO. I am worried about you Lizzy.

LIZZY. *(Softly.)* I'm worried about me too.

DONNA JO. What's goin' on with you?

LIZZY. *(Hesitant.)* It's everything...everything is a disaster–

>(**DONNA JO** *and* **BECCA** *lean in.*)

BECCA.	**DONNA JO.**
Well...go on...spill –	Let's hear it.

LIZZY. I mean... Bobby is wonderful...but...well...okay... maybe he's not so wonderful... I mean... *(Deep breath.)* Girls...my life isn't as perfect as I let on.

DONNA JO. SHOCKER!! *(Beat.)* Whose is Lizzy?

LIZZY. *(Flood.)* Y'all... Bobby hasn't worked in almost two years. He spends most of his days on the golf course waitin' for his phone to ring. He says all the good jobs are taken and he's holdin' out for a *(Air quotes.)* "*supervisor's position.*" *(Beat.)* Bobby can't even supervise his own underwear drawer.

BECCA. Oh Lizzy...why didn't you –

LIZZY. Meantime, here I am...runnin' all over hell and half of Georgia...tryin' to drum up business for the Miss Georgia Belle pageants, just to pay the bills. *(Beat.)* I've started makin' up pageant titles just so I can hold more contests. *(Beat.)* Next month I'm havin' the Little Miss Georgia Belle Pre-Teen Plus-Sized Starlet of America Pageant...so I can try to catch up on all our credit card bills. *(Beat.)* Girls... I'm afraid we're gonna lose the house.

BECCA. Oh Elizabeth, I –

LIZZY. And the twins are a complete nightmare from hell. The entire house is covered in toothpaste and urine... and they're fightin' all the time...stealin' my car... robbin' my purse...gettin' suspended from school...the principal has me on speed dial. We shoulda' named 'em Cain and Abel...because I swear...one of them will eventually kill the other one.

DONNA JO. I thought you said they were doin' real good –

LIZZY. Oh sweetie... I lied...they're both juvenile delinquents...there's not a whole brain between the two of them. I'm just prayin' we can get them through air conditionin' repair school and keep them from becomin' ditch diggers...or politicians. *(Beat.)*

BECCA. I had no idea –

DONNA JO. I'm sorry to hear all this Lizzy... I really am... but...sugar you have gotta go –

LIZZY. What? But I just...

DONNA JO. Caroline is not ready to deal with you right now and –

*(**CAROLINE** steps into the doorway.)*

CAROLINE. No...stop Donna Jo...it's okay. *(Beat.)* Hi Lizzy –

(**LIZZY** *rushes to* **CAROLINE**.)

LIZZY. *(Relieved.)* Hi –

CAROLINE. Hi Lizzy –

LIZZY. Oh, Caroline... I'm so sorry –

CAROLINE. No...no... Lizzy... *I'm* sorry –

(**LIZZY** *and* **CAROLINE** *embrace.* **CAROLINE** *gestures for* **BECCA** *and* **DONNA JO** *to leave.*)

DONNA JO. *(Bad acting.)* Oh...well...hmmm *(Checks her watch.)* It's almost time for me to get into my costume for the show tonight. Luckily... I brought it with me... so... I guess I'll just go into the bedroom now and put that on...so I can get to the show on time. *(Beat.)* Oh Becca...would you come help me...with my...uh...hair and makeup?

BECCA. Sure, Donna Jo... I'll help you...with your costume...and your hair...or somethin'...sure...yeah... you betcha' –

(**DONNA JO** *and* **BECCA** *exit right.*)

LIZZY. That was believable.

CAROLINE. Lizzy... I heard everything –

LIZZY. Oh Caroline... I'm sorry I acted like a complete –

CAROLINE. Temporarily?

(They giggle.)

You are one of the strongest and boldest women I know. Why have you let Bobby and the boys get away with this for so long?

LIZZY. I don't know... I guess I've been in denial... I want everything to be perfect...so I try to ignore all the ugliness and –

CAROLINE. You mean you want things to *appear* to be perfect...on the outside –

LIZZY. What?

CAROLINE. Lizzy... I spent my entire childhood tryin' to be the best at everything. I wanted...no... I *needed*...my life to look perfect –

LIZZY. Your life was about as perfect as they get.

CAROLINE. No...no it wasn't. Momma and I just made it look that way.

LIZZY. What are you talkin' about?

CAROLINE. Oh Lizzy...there is so much you don't know. *(Beat.)* Things I've never told anyone –

LIZZY. There's something I need to tell you too. *(Beat.)* But But I don't even know where to start –

CAROLINE. I'm so sorry I was such an overachiever back in high school...and I'm sorry I left... I wish I could go back and change it...but I can't.

LIZZY. What do you mean?

CAROLINE. Lizzy...Momma made me promise that I wouldn't –

> *(Suddenly, **BECCA** and **DONNA JO** scream from offstage.)*

LIZZY.	**CAROLINE.**
What in the world?	Oh Lord!

> *(**DONNA JO** runs in, frantic. She is dressed in a black dress, witch's hat with attached black hair, a green half-witch mask and black cape.)*

DONNA JO. *(Terror.)* HELP... CALL 911... CALL AN AMBULANCE... CALL THE NATIONAL GUARD! *(Puzzled beat.)* Is the room spinning? Is it hot in here?

CAROLINE. What in the world Donna Jo?

LIZZY. What in the *hell* are you wearin'?

DONNA JO. It's Becca...she's...she's having the...oh... I feel dizzy... I feel like I'm gonna –

    *(**DONNA JO** faints on the sofa. **LIZZY** and **CAROLINE** rush to her.)*

CAROLINE. DONNA JO... DONNA JO! *(Then.)* Lizzy go get a cold cloth.

    *(**LIZZY** runs to the kitchen sink, as **BECCA** waddles in casually applying lip gloss.)*

BECCA. *(Mildly pained.)* Well y'all...my water just broke... y'all are gonna have to get me to the hospital. How does my makeup look? *(She looks into a compact.)* If you were a hot, single obstetrician...would you date me? *(Beat.)* Oh lord...what happened to Donna Jo?

    *(**LIZZY** gives the cloth to **CAROLINE**. She dabs it on **DONNA JO**'s neck.)*

CAROLINE. She fainted.

BECCA. *(Impatient.)* Of course she did...*drama queen*... did she hit her head?

CAROLINE. No...I don't think –

BECCA. Good...how do I look?

LIZZY.	**CAROLINE.**
Oh...yeah Rebecca... you're lookin' totally hot.	Super-dooper cute.

    *(**BECCA** cries out with a contraction. **DONNA JO** rouses.)*

DONNA JO. What's happenin'? Did I miss my entrance? *(She reaches out dramatically.)* I'll get you my pretty and your little dog too –

CAROLINE. *(Exasperated.)* You fainted Donna Jo…and Becca is in labor.

LIZZY. I'll go start the car. Do you want me to call Tucker?

>   *(**LIZZY** grabs her purse and starts to the front door.)*

BECCA. WHAT? NO! How am I gonna get a date with *him* there? *(Beat.)* But, will you call Momma please… tell her to bring the girls… I told them they could see little Magnolia be born. Oh… Donna Jo…grab my bag please and get the video camera.

DONNA JO. *(Faint gasp.)* What?

BECCA. My *bag*…my bag…grab my bag… I want you to record the birth…the video camera is in my bag.

>   *(**DONNA JO** faints again.)*

LIZZY. *(Eye roll.)* Don't worry darlin'… I'll record it *(Then aside.)* God help me –

>   *(**LIZZY** grabs **DONNA JO**'s bag and exits. **CAROLINE** fans and tries to rouse **DONNA JO**.)*

CAROLINE. DONNA JO! Becca needs us…you have got to get it together honey.

BECCA. *(Modeling.)* Caroline…how's my hair? Is it good?

CAROLINE. It's a little flat in the back…wait…what am I sayin'?

>   *(We hear a car start and the car horn honk. **DONNA JO** rouses.)*

DONNA JO. What? OK…yeah…okay… I'm ready…let's do this.

>   *(**DONNA JO** jumps up and grabs **BECCA** around the chest from behind, attempting to lift her and drag her towards the door.)*

BECCA. What are you doing wacko? Stop it –

DONNA JO. I'm helpin' you to the car. Don't worry y'all... I got this... I played a nurse in a TV commercial for Savannah General Hospital –

CAROLINE. Donna Jo... I think Becca can walk to the car.

BECCA. YES... I CAN –

>   (**LIZZY** *enters.*)

LIZZY. OK the car is started and...

>   (**LIZZY** *sees* **DONNA JO** *trying to lift* **BECCA** *and panic sets in.*)

LIZZY. OH NO...what happened... Did she pass out...let me help you... Becca...don't worry, sugar...it's gonna be OK... I called your momma...she's on the way –

>   (**LIZZY** *grabs* **BECCA***'s feet and begins to help* **DONNA JO** *lift/carry* **BECCA** *to the door. They lift her completely into the air as she struggles.*)

BECCA.	**CAROLINE.**
STOP IT Y'ALL... I CAN WALK –	Y'all stop... STOP!

>   (**DONNA JO, LIZZY,** *and* **CAROLINE** *argue as they struggle back and forth from the door to the sofa.* **BECCA** *is screaming and is eventually "dropped" behind the sofa.*)

BECCA. Lordamercy...are y'all tryin' to kill me?

>   (**BECCA** *pulls herself up over the back of the sofa.* **LIZZY** *and* **DONNA JO** *go to help her up and she swats them away*)

I'm fine...let's just go to the car. *(Beat.)* Y'all prob'ly messed up my hair.

(**BECCA** *pulls out her mirror to check her hair.*)

DONNA JO. Y'all are gonna have to take me to theatre…the show starts at seven thirty.

LIZZY. Why don't you just fly there…on your broom?

CAROLINE. Yeah…what about that? I thought you were playin' Dorothy –

DONNA JO. Yeah… So I guess y'all –

(**BECCA** *cries out again.*)

BECCA. EXCUSE ME… HELLO! Woman in labor! Somebody grab me a towel to sit on in the car…and bring the blender… 'cause I'm gonna be ready for a drink, the second I get the O-K.

CAROLINE. I don't think that's how it works darlin'.

BECCA. That's how it's gonna work for me…let's go.

(**LIZZY** *grabs the blender.* **CAROLINE** *grabs a towel from the console and brings it to* **BECCA.**)

LIZZY. Towel…check. Video camera…check. Blender…check. What else?

BECCA. *(Strained.)* Tequila!

(**DONNA JO** *grabs the tequila from the kitchen table and holds it up.*)

DONNA JO. TEQUILA, CHECK!!!

(**LIZZY** *and* **DONNA JO** *exit.* **BECCA** *is looking in her compact.*)

BECCA. Sweetie… I left some of my makeup in the bathroom…can you grab it? I need mascara.

CAROLINE. Sure darlin'. Oooo…just think…in a few hours you're gonna be holdin' your baby!

*(**CAROLINE** exits.)*

BECCA. *(Loud.)* No ma'am...my momma's gonna be holdin' that baby... *I'M* gonna be holdin' a margarita! *(Calling out.)* I CALL SHOTGUN!!!

*(**BECCA** exits as **CAROLINE** calls out.)*

CAROLINE. Where is it Becca? I can't find it...all I see is... *(Beat.)* Oh wait...never mind...here it is.

*(**CAROLINE** reenters.)*

Hello?

(She crosses to get her purse...muttering "I can't believe this." "Why me?" etc. She crosses to the front door, then turns back, looks up and shakes her finger.)

(Stern.) I can hear you Momma... STOP LAUGHIN'!

(She exits.)

(Blackout.)

Scene Two

(One week later. A peppy gospel song with a female lead, plays on the stereo.* The sofa is covered in a paint tarp. The rotary phone is on the stereo console. A pitcher of margaritas is on the coffee table with four red party cups. The scrapbook is on the coffee table. Miss Polly's urn sits on the coffee table beside a framed picture of her. Caroline's DO NOT DONATE box, sits on the console. **DONNA JO** *and* **LIZZY** *enter right. They are wearing oversized men's shirts with paint and black tire marks on the back of them. They carry paint rollers and a gallon bucket of paint or other painting supplies.)*

DONNA JO. All we need to do is touch up the trim around the ceilin' in the bathroom and that side of the house will *finally* be finished.

LIZZY. When are they bringin' the new carpet?

DONNA JO. Next Tuesday.

LIZZY. I'm so glad Caroline decided to listen to the realtor and give the house a little facelift before she puts it on the market.

DONNA JO. *(Sarcastic.)* Oh yeah…me too…because this is soooo much fun.

*(**LIZZY** crosses and turns off the music.)*

LIZZY. Tucker's shirts worked out great for paintin' smocks. I'm glad these didn't get burned up with all his other stuff.

---

* A license to produce *Packing Up Polly* does not include a performance license for any third-party or copyrighted music. Licensees should create an original composition or use music in the public domain. For further information, please see the Music and Third-Party Materials Use Note on page iii.

(**LIZZY** *turns around and there are black tire marks across the back of her lightly-burned shirt.*)

DONNA JO. Yes... I'm glad they survived your *Fatal Attraction* rampage too.

(*They pause and look around.*)

(*Huff.*) OK...so what color are we paintin' in here?

LIZZY. Blue... I think.

(**CAROLINE** *enters. She is carrying a paint bucket and paintbrush. She also wears an oversized men's shirt with paint and tire marks on it.*)

CAROLINE. It's called Serenity Blue. It's a soft...calming color. The kitchen will be the same color.

(*We hear a car horn.*)

DONNA JO. (*Calling off stage.*) BECCA... YOUR MOMMA IS –

(**BECCA** *runs in. She is wearing a bright, sassy outfit. She has a car baby carrier, diaper bag, and a baby bottle.*)

BECCA. (*Loud.*) THANK YOU JESUS!!! I'm comin' Momma –

(**BECCA** *runs out the front door.*)

CAROLINE. Becca's momma is a *saint*.

DONNA JO. The shine wore off that penny awful quick... what's it been, three days?

CAROLINE. Stop it...it's been a week –

LIZZY. This is number five... I'm sure the thrill is gone.

DONNA JO. Five children...makes my head spin thinkin' about it.

LIZZY. Two has just about killed me.

> (**DONNA JO** *crosses to the coffee table.*)

DONNA JO. Who wants another margarita?

CAROLINE.	**LIZZY.**
Yes please.	You don't have to ask me twice.

> (*They cross to the sofa.* **DONNA JO** *pours.* **BECCA** *returns, still holding the baby bottle.*)

BECCA. BYE MOMMA... THANK YOU!

> (*We hear a car driving away and horn – beep beep.*)

Did I hear margaritas?

DONNA JO. OK now wait...when you had that first one... you told us to remind you *not* to have any more.

LIZZY. You said if you pick up *anything* fattenin' –

CAROLINE. – that we are supposed to slap it out of your mouth.

> (**BECCA** *glares at them.*)

BECCA. I hate you all.

LIZZY. You said you wanted to lose the baby weight.

BECCA. Yeah yeah... I know...but...if I *don't* lose it...it'll be harder for someone to kidnap me...so *hit me bartender*.

> (**BECCA** *raises her cup.* **DONNA JO** *pours.* **BECCA** *is still holding a baby bottle.*)

CAROLINE. Becca...you forgot to give your momma the bottle.

BECCA. CRAP! ...I've been pumpin' all mornin'!

(**BECCA** *crosses to put the bottle in the refrigerator, then turns back.*)

I'm considerin' changin' my name to Beulah the cow. *(Beat.)* Eh...she has seven more in the diaper bag.

DONNA JO. Well, I don't know about you two, but I'm not waitin' another second to ask. *(Beat.)* Becca...what is goin' on with you and doctor cutie wootie patootie?

BECCA. *(Schoolgirl.)* His name is David.

DONNA JO. Yeah yeah...okay...so...did he really ask you out?

LIZZY. How is that even possible? Is that *legal*?

BECCA. *(Innocent.)* I don't know... I just happened to mention that Tucker and I were gettin' a divorce –

DONNA JO. You *mentioned* it at least a dozen times between contractions –

(**BECCA** *gives* **DONNA JO** *the stink eye.*)

BECCA. *As I was sayin'...* I mentioned that I was gettin' a divorce...and...he just...you know...asked me out.

LIZZY. What I want to know...is how it went from "ONE MORE PUSH" to... "Hey babe...wanna go out some time?"

BECCA. Stop it...stop teasin' me...y'all know he didn't deliver the baby.

DONNA JO. I still can't believe Doctor Dixon hobbled in on his one good foot and delivered little Magnolia.

BECCA. *(Adamant.)* ...and David delivered *another baby* in the next room.

CAROLINE. I have to admit...he is one good lookin' man... and a doctor to boot...

DONNA JO. Oh yeah...you go girl!

LIZZY. Well, the divorce is final next month...so...you will finally be free.

CAROLINE. Did Tucker finally get all his stuff out of the house?

BECCA. Yeah...there wasn't much left after Lizzy set it all on fire...but what was left, he took to his room over at the mo-tel.

DONNA JO. He's not shacked up with his little Lolita?

BECCA. OH THAT'S RIGHT! I didn't tell y'all. *(Dramatic pause.)* SHE DUMPED HIM!!!

| **DONNA JO.** | **LIZZY.** | **CAROLINE.** |
| NO! | Shut up! | Are you serious? |

BECCA. Yes...well...it seems that sweet, Double D Tiffany's idea of a good time, does *not* include a herd of screamin' kids, a cryin' baby, and a sack of Krystal burgers at the Mo-tel 6.

DONNA JO, CAROLINE & LIZZY. *(Fake sympathy.)* Awwwww

*(The telephone rings. **CAROLINE** answers.)*

CAROLINE. Hello... Chelsea? Where are you? *(Beat.)* What? No...it's not. Where's Michael? ...Are you serious? *(Appalled.)* What do you mean... *I'm takin' too long*?

*(**LIZZY** storms to the phone, snatching it from **CAROLINE**.)*

LIZZY. Chelsea Porter...now you listen to me you little gold-diggin' sack of silicone... I am just about sick to death of...hello... HELLO? *(Beat.)* She hung up on you again...she is so *rude*.

BECCA. Did she just tell you that you're takin' too long with the house?

CAROLINE. She did –

DONNA JO. And where is Michael?

CAROLINE. I have no idea –

BECCA. Miss Polly obviously didn't swat those fannies enough.

DONNA JO. It's never too late... I'll swat 'em for ya'.

BECCA. I'll help...go pick me a switch –

> (**CAROLINE** *crosses to the sofa and sits.*)

CAROLINE. This is a mess...everything is a mess...this is too fast. (**CAROLINE** *looks up.*) I'm sorry Momma... I'm so sorry.

> (**CAROLINE** *begins to cry. Everyone surrounds her for comfort.*)

DONNA JO.	**BECCA.**	**LIZZY.**
Oh sweetie...it's okay.	Oh, precious girl.	Let it out Caroline.

CAROLINE. I can't believe I've done this to my momma... I promised her I'd keep everything perfect...and now I've just thrown out everything she loved.

LIZZY. Caroline...you know your momma didn't really *love* all this *junk*...she just couldn't help herself...it's a...a... disorder... I saw it on Dr. Oz.

CAROLINE. All this *junk*...put up a wall between me and Momma...and kept her from movin' up to Atlanta...she wouldn't...or *couldn't*...get rid of anything...and it just kept pilin' up.

BECCA. What do you mean...you had to keep things perfect?

CAROLINE. Momma had secrets –

DONNA JO, BECCA & LIZZY. Secrets?

> (**DONNA JO, LIZZY** *and* **BECCA** *lean in.*)

CAROLINE. Well... I guess I may as well tell y'all. No use in keepin' secrets anymore. *(Heavy beat and cross. She looks up.)* I love you Momma. *(Beat.)* My father wasn't the good Christian my momma was. *(Beat.)* He was a gamblin', cheatin', alcoholic that left us when I was five.

DONNA JO. Oh Caroline...how awful.

LIZZY. *(Shock.)* I thought your daddy died in a car accident.

BECCA. Me too.

CAROLINE. That's what Momma told everybody when we moved here...you know how the Baptists frown on divorce...it was better that she was a widow...but the truth is...last I heard...he's somewhere in Texas...or Mexico –

BECCA. Caroline...that's awful... I'm so sorry...we didn't know.

CAROLINE. *No one* knows...not even Chelsea and Michael. I've never told anyone...until now...Momma made me promise –

LIZZY. Oh Caroline –

CAROLINE. So, I always felt like I had to be the best at everything...to make Momma happy and to keep the secret.

DONNA JO. What a terrible cross to bear –

LIZZY. Caroline...we were like sisters... I wish you'd told me.

CAROLINE. Things are different now Lizzy...but back then...if people found out...it would have been a big scandal. Polly Porter and The Praise His Name Singers would have been over...and Momma needed that money to raise us. *(Beat.)* That's why I left Savannah. I just couldn't go on livin' that lie anymore...or deal with all her...hoardin'.

LIZZY. All those years...feelin' like I was standin' in your shadow...feelin' so jealous of all those trophies and crowns...and you were hidin' all that pain –

CAROLINE. *Jealous?* Of *me?* *(Beat.) OH LIZZY...* I was jealous of *you.* You were popular and beautiful... everybody loved you. You were a rock star Lizzy...you still are!

*(**CAROLINE** faces **LIZZY** and takes her hands.)*

LIZZY. Well...this might change your mind –

CAROLINE. Huh?

LIZZY. *(Nervous.)* Caroline...back in high school... I had a crush...on Patrick... I mean...nothin' happened...but... not because I didn't try... I mean... I knew he liked you...but –

DONNA JO. *Everybody* knew that Lizzy.

BECCA. I didn't –

CAROLINE. Lizzy...you don't need to –

LIZZY. Anyway...you know that night at the drive-in... when we locked Donna Jo in the trunk and y'all couldn't find me? It's because I was...in the backseat of his Mustang...tryin' to get him to...*you know*...with me –

CAROLINE. Oh Lizzy...don't –

LIZZY. *(Bitter.)* All he could talk about...was *you* Caroline. There I was...draped across his backseat...and all he could talk about...was you...and if I thought you might go out with him –

CAROLINE. *(Tearful.)* Oh Lizzy... I didn't know...I'm sorry.

LIZZY. *(Tearful.)* I know... I know. I'm so sorry too Caroline.

CAROLINE. No...no...sweetie –

(They embrace.)

BECCA. *(Crying.)* Ooooo... I wanna be sorry for somethin' too!

DONNA JO. *(Weepy.)* ME TOO!

CAROLINE. Well come on in here then –

> *(**DONNA JO** and **BECCA** join in a group hug for a giant ball of love and tears. **DONNA JO** pulls away first.)*

DONNA JO. So listen y'all...maybe now, is a good time to talk about the elephant in the room?

BECCA. What elephant?

DONNA JO. The...uh...Patrick elephant.

BECCA. Uh...yeah...soooooo speakin' of Patrick –

> *(Everyone looks at **CAROLINE**.)*

CAROLINE. *(Resigned.)* Yeah...okay...so... Patrick and I... well...we're...gettin' a divorce.

> *(**DONNA JO**, **BECCA** and **LIZZY** all feign shock.)*

| **BECCA.** | **LIZZY.** | **DONNA JO.** |
| Oh no...really? | I'm shocked | Nooooooooo |

> *(**CAROLINE** rolls her eyes and then they all snicker.)*

CAROLINE. Look...girls...it's OK ...there's no big drama... we've just grown apart. We still love each other...we're family...but we've finally faced the facts. We got married for all the wrong reasons. *(Beat.)* I wanted out of Savannah so bad, I woulda' married *anyone* headin' out of town...and Patrick... Patrick just wanted to do what everyone expected...marry the Head Cheerleader and become a success. We've been livin' separate lives in the same house for years...and now...now we're fixin' it.

DONNA JO. I'm so sorry Caroline.

CAROLINE. Patrick was comin' to Momma's funeral...but I told him he didn't need to...that I needed to do this...alone.

LIZZY. Well...how did that work out for ya?

(Everyone laughs and moves to the sofa.)

BECCA. Well...seems like we've all had bad luck in the men department...one way or the other.

DONNA JO. Lord knows I have –

*(**BECCA** picks up the scrapbook and opens it.)*

LIZZY. What happened to us? We were so *bold...so strong* and we shared so many dreams together.

(Beat.)

CAROLINE. *(Resigned.)* I've forgotten what it's like to have a dream.

BECCA. *(Distant.)* Sometimes I dream that Tucker falls off a cliff. *(Then.)* Oh wait...did I just say that out loud?

DONNA JO. There's still time girls...we're not dead yet –

CAROLINE. You know...Momma used to say...it's never too late to live happily ever after.

LIZZY. *(Excited.)* Maybe we should try to...no...no –

CAROLINE. What?

LIZZY. Nothin'.

BECCA. Oh. My. Stars...would you look at this –

*(**BECCA** pulls a photo out of the scrapbook. **DONNA JO** takes it from her.)*

DONNA JO. *(Laughing.)* STOP!!! Look at this y'all! This is the Little Miss Sassy Savannah Pageant.

BECCA. Was I in that one?

DONNA JO. No...just Lizzy and Caroline...but I was there. We were in the fourth grade.

CAROLINE. How do you remember these things?

DONNA JO. How could I forget? Lizzy's momma raised a big ole stink when Lizzy didn't win. She threw one of Lizzy's tap shoes at a judge... Nancy Beth Brady...hit her right between the eyes and knocked her out cold. People were hidin' up under chairs.

LIZZY. That did *not* happen –

DONNA JO. Nancy Beth has a scar on her forehead to prove it –

> (**LIZZY** *takes* **CAROLINE***'s hand.* **BECCA** *discovers an envelope in the back of the scrapbook. Unnoticed by the others, she begins to read it silently...eyes widening.*)

LIZZY. Caroline...c'mon...let's chase our dreams... together...let's open that Beauty Pageant Cheerleadin' School.

DONNA JO. *(Reminding.)* And dancin' and baton twirlin' –

LIZZY. Come home Caroline...come back to Savannah.

DONNA JO. Oh yes –

CAROLINE. Girls...after the divorce...I was gonna move back down here to take care of Momma...but now... I don't know –

LIZZY. You just said Miss Polly told you it's never too late to live happily ever after.

CAROLINE. Lizzy...my life is a wreck...and *your* life is a wreck. I don't think I –

LIZZY. All the more reason –

CAROLINE. Where are we gonna get the money? You're broke as a church mouse...and I'm not exactly rollin' in the dough.

> (**BECCA** gasps loudly as her mouth falls open.)

BECCA. OH YES YOU ARE!!!

> (**BECCA** excitedly passes the papers to **CAROLINE**.)

CAROLINE. What is this?

> (Everyone gathers around. Eyes widen...there are gasps...mouths fall open. **CAROLINE** flips the pages and reads. Her eyes flood with tears and she passes the papers to **LIZZY**.)

No... I can't... I can't...here...you read it.

DONNA JO.	**LIZZY.**
Oh Caroline.	Is this real?

> (**LIZZY** silently reads the paper for a second, then begins to read aloud.)

LIZZY. Dear Caroline... Well my darlin'...chances are, if you're readin' this... I have gone on up to heaven to be with Jesus. *(Beat.)* I know you'll be sortin' through the house, so I decided to put this letter in your scrapbook... because I know with all my clutter...you'll find it here.

There are so many things I wish I could have changed Caroline. I know that your childhood was difficult and that it wasn't easy to keep all our secrets. I asked so much of you...and I missed so much. Thank you for always bein' there for me. Thank you for lovin' me. Thank you for always takin' care of your brother and sister...and bein' the best daughter a momma could ever ask for.

My beautiful girl...as you can see, I've left most everything for you. I gave some to the church and left a little bit for Chelsea and Michael...and put away the rest for you...includin' the house, my jewelry, and the royalties to all my music. Don't worry about your brother and sister contestin' the will...they don't have the sense God gave a goose...and besides...they have already gotten more than their share while I was alive. As it is...you are set for life...no matter what that life is...you will be comfortable for the rest of it. Now close your mouth darlin'... I know you thought I spent it all on my stuff...but as you can see...there is plenty left and then some.

I want you to make all your dreams come true...with or without Patrick...and remember...it's never too late to live happily ever after.

I love you precious girl...a bushel and a peck and a hug around the neck...forever... Momma.

P.S. ...I hope you can reconnect with the girls...and when you do...give them a big ole hug...from their Momma Polly.

*(**CAROLINE** takes the papers.)*

CAROLINE. This is dated last month...right after she came up to see me in Atlanta and I asked her to move up there with me.

*(**DONNA JO** takes the papers.)*

DONNA JO. That is a lot of money Caroline... I mean... *A LOT.*

BECCA. It is –

LIZZY. And the house...the house too.

DONNA JO. *(Still staring at the paper.)* That is *a lot* of zeros.

*(**CAROLINE** crosses to the kitchen and then turns back, scanning the room.)*

CAROLINE. Well girls... I guess I'm gonna have to figure out how to fit all my furniture in here.

*(**DONNA JO**, **BECCA** and **LIZZY** gasp and jump up screaming.)*

BECCA. OOOO I think I just tinkled a little.

DONNA JO.	**LIZZY**.
Are you serious?	Caroline...really?

CAROLINE. Now don't get overly excited...it's not gonna happen tomorrow...but...it is time for me to make a fresh start –

LIZZY. And we can help you make it –

CAROLINE. ...and we've got a lot of time to make up for... and dreams to share...remember?

DONNA JO. Does this mean the beauty twirlin' pageant school thingy is happenin'?

BECCA. I'll send ya five customers right off the bat...and Tucker will pay for it.

CAROLINE. *(Smiling.)* OK...let's do this girls –

LIZZY. *(Sudden frenzy.)* OOOOO OK! So we gotta find a location...and we need a lotta space...like warehouse. OH... and we gotta come up with a name... I've always thought *"Beautiful Little Divas Twirl and Cheer"* is a good name...what do y'all think? Maybe *"Cheer and Dance"* or *"Cheer and Pose"*...anyway...we'll work on it. Oh...and...maybe we can get Libby Maison to teach dance –

DONNA JO. Oooo...and I can teach actin' –

BECCA. I'll answer the phones...and make the margaritas–

LIZZY. *(Building.)* And then...after a couple of years...we can franchise it out...and have locations *all* over the South...and then the whole country...and then after that...we can go global...and –

CAROLINE. LIZZY!!! Stop! Lordamercy...you're gettin' all...well...you know –

> *(**LIZZY** stops and whips around. She gives **CAROLINE** "the look." A silence falls over the room.)*

LIZZY. Excuse me? What are you tryin' to say Caroline?

> *(**LIZZY** and **CAROLINE** glare at each other... then, **CAROLINE** laughs as she takes **LIZZY**'s hand. Everyone laughs, relieved.)*

BECCA. OK...well... I for one am about to starve to death... and believe it or not...we have *finally* run out of fried chicken. Who wants to make a Burger Barn run?

DONNA JO. Me!!!

BECCA. I mean...my butt is saying "no"...but my mouth is saying "yes please"...*and* we also need to stop at the liquor store too –

> *(**DONNA JO**, **BECCA** and **LIZZY** start grabbing their purses and head to the door.)*

CAROLINE. OH wait...wait Lizzy... I have somethin' I want to give you.

> *(**CAROLINE** goes to the box on the console and takes out a rhinestone crown. She crosses to **LIZZY**.)*

LIZZY. What? Why?

CAROLINE. Because...you're a queen...and you deserve a crown –

(**CAROLINE** *places the crown on* **LIZZY***'s head and takes her face in her hands. She kisses her cheek.* **LIZZY** *begins to "walk the runway" and wave like a beauty queen as* **DONNA JO** *sings."**)

DONNA JO.
 HEEEERE SHE IIIISSSSSS...LITTLE MISS CRAAAAAZY PANTS...

CAROLINE. I love you sweet friend...and I love you girls too.

(*She giggles and pulls two more crowns from the box.*)

Here...have a crown (*She mimics Oprah Winfrey.*) You get a crown, and you get a crown...everyone gets a crown!

BECCA. I love it!

(**DONNA JO** *and* **BECCA** *giggle as they take their crowns and put them on their heads.*)

DONNA JO. OK...come on... I don't have much time before I have to get down to the little theatre.

LIZZY. Yeah...about that Witchy Poo...what happened to you playin' Dorothy?

DONNA JO. I'm not a complete idiot... I know I may be a little mature for that role...and anyway...y'all know how I love to scare little kids...so...it's a win-win really. Besides...there are much juicer older roles for me... like...Sandy in *Grease* or Gypsy Rose Lee.

BECCA. I'm pretty sure they're also younger than –

---

* A license to produce *Packing Up Polly* does not include a performance license for any third-party or copyrighted music. Licensees should create an original composition or use music in the public domain. For further information, please see the Music and Third-Party Materials Use Note on page iii.

DONNA JO. BABY STEPS! OK? *(Beat.)* Anyway...y'all are ALL comin' to see the last show tonight.

LIZZY. *(Mutter.)* I'm gonna have a severe migraine at around that time...sorry –

BECCA. Whatever...let's go go go –

DONNA JO. I hope I don't see anybody I know...I look like I've been run over by a car.

CAROLINE. *(Giggle.)* Well...you kinda were –

LIZZY. OK EVERYBODY...let's do this... PORK CHOP CHEER... READY!? OK! PORK CHOP PORK CHOP GREASY GREASY... WE CAN BEAT YOUR TEAM... EASY EASY!

> *(**BECCA** and **DONNA JO** join in. **LIZZY** exits first, then **DONNA JO** and **BECCA** last. As **BECCA** begins to exit, she turns back.)*

BECCA. Let's go Caroline...

CAROLINE. Start the car and I'll be there in a second.

> *(**BECCA** exits...joining the cheer...as it fades. **CAROLINE** crosses to the coffee table and picks up the papers. She folds them and puts them back in the scrapbook. She crosses to put the scrapbook in the box and finds another crown. She giggles and starts to put the crown on her head...then pauses...looking at the urn. She smiles...then crosses and places it around the urn.)*

Well Momma...you did it. Thank you... I love you Momma...a bushel and a peck and a hug around the neck...forever and ever.

> *(**CAROLINE** rises, kisses her hand, and touches the top of the urn...smiling and lingering for a moment...then takes her purse and crosses to the front door.)*

CAROLINE. OK girls...let's go... PORK CHOP PORK CHOP GREASY GREASY... WE CAN BEAT YOUR –

*(**CAROLINE**'s voice fades with the lights.)*

(Blackout.)

End of Play

www.ingramcontent.com/pod-product-compliance
Lightning Source LLC
LaVergne TN
LVHW010417030825
817679LV00043B/1236